THE HEEL OF ACHILLES

'*I'm done for . . . find X.1 . . . Dene . . . You must . . . Tooth-paste . . .* '
England is at war with Germany and Dene of the Secret Service tries to decipher his fatally wounded colleague's garbled message — potentially vital information for England's survival. Who is X.1? What does the word *Tooth-paste* signify? Dene must find out and stop X.1, or the Third Reich will strike a crippling blow to England and change the course of the war. And he has just eight days in which to do it . . .

Books by Gerald Verner
in the Linford Mystery Library:

THE LAST WARNING
DENE OF THE SECRET SERVICE
THE NURSERY RHYME MURDERS
TERROR TOWER
THE CLEVERNESS OF MR. BUDD
THE SEVEN LAMPS
THEY WALK IN DARKNESS

GERALD VERNER

THE HEEL OF ACHILLES

Complete and Unabridged

LINFORD
Leicester

First published in Great Britain

First Linford Edition
published 2011

British Library CIP Data

Verner, Gerald.
  The heel of Achilles.- -
  (Linford mystery library)
  1. World War, *1939 – 1945*- -Secret service- -
  Great Britain- -Fiction. 2. Spy stories.
  3. Large type books.
  I. Title II. Series
  823.9'12–dc22

  ISBN 978–1–4448–0855–1

Published by
F. A. Thorpe (Publishing)
Anstey, Leicestershire

Set by Words & Graphics Ltd.
Anstey, Leicestershire
Printed and bound in Great Britain by
T. J. International Ltd., Padstow, Cornwall

This book is printed on acid-free paper

FOR
CAROL

Foreword

This book was completed in the early part of 1944. Since then considerable changes have taken place in the war with Germany and the outcome has completely altered. The period during which the events recorded in this novel took place was, however, before these momentous happenings occurred.

It might also be as well to state that all the characters, places, and incidents in this story are entirely fictitious and have no relation to any person, places, or incidents in real life.

GERALD VERNER.

March, 1945.

1

Friday — Midnight

A coal fell noisily into the grate, and the Reverend Colgate-Jones looked up from his untidy writing-table, a frown on his round, florid face. Laying down his pen, he sat back in the shabby desk-chair and gently rubbed the top of his bald head.

He was trying to prepare his sermon for the coming Sunday, but his efforts up to now had not been very successful. Two hours' hard concentration had resulted in an appreciable addition to the queer little sketches which ornamented the blotting-pad, but nothing else.

With a grunt of disgust he rose wearily to his feet, crossed over to the fireplace, and began to fill his pipe. It was still raining heavily — he could hear the hiss and splash of it on the trees and gravel outside — and the wind had risen. It had been raining steadily all day, a ceaseless

1

downpour from a sky the colour of lead, and, from the look of it, would probably rain all day tomorrow, too. A depressing prospect.

Colgate-Jones sighed, lit his pipe, flicked the used match into the fire, and sat down in an armchair by the hearth. It was nearly twelve o'clock, but he had no particular desire to go to bed. A restlessness which he knew of old had taken possession of him — an intense craving for something to happen, anything that would break the deadly monotony of the daily round.

Behind the rotund and placid exterior of the Reverend Colgate-Jones lurked a spirit of adventure that few of his parishioners even guessed at, and which would certainly have horrified his Bishop had that worthy, but unimaginative, man even dimly suspected that it existed. It was a queer boyish love of excitement that found little outlet in the dull routine duties of a village clergyman. There *had* been a brief interlude, a long time ago it seemed now, when that love of excitement had been amply gratified. When each day

2

had brought with it a fresh danger and a fresh problem; when all his wits had been tested hourly to keep alive.

He let himself think back to the time of the queer business of Norris Jordan and the Seven Clues,[*] and that gloriously dangerous month in midsummer when he had shared with Peter Clayton and Michael Dene the perils and triumphs connected with the overthrow of Morgan Stenson and his satellites. Many things had happened since then. There had been wars and rumours of wars, and finally WAR in capital letters. Peter Clayton was in Egypt; Michael Dene appeared to have vanished from the face of the earth. There had been no sign or word from him for many months. As head of the Special Branch of the British Intelligence Department he was probably pretty busy just now . . .

Colgate-Jones pinched the loose skin between his brows and wrinkled his nose. Everybody had their jobs to do and if some were less spectacular than others, they were

---

[*] The Seven Clues.

equally as important. His job, as Vicar of Claybury, might be dull, but it was . . .

He stopped in the midst of his musing to listen. From somewhere outside in the dark wetness of the night he thought he had heard a faint cry. It might have been a distant owl or some other night bird — they sounded curiously human at times — but it had sounded to him like a cry for help.

Pipe in hand he got up and went over to the window. Slipping behind the heavy blackout curtains he peered through the rain-blurred glass into darkness. He could see nothing. The splashing of the rain and the ripple of the river, which flowed along the bottom of the vicarage garden, were the only sounds that reached him. The cry, if it *had* been a cry, was not repeated.

After listening intently for a minute or so, he came back to the fire, glancing automatically at the clock on the mantelpiece. Midnight. High time he was in bed. His niece, who had been bombed out of her flat in London and was staying with him, had been in bed and asleep for

4

some time like a sensible girl. His housekeeper and the maid had long since retired. Only he was up, wasting his time in foolish and unprofitable retrospection.

Firmly he knocked the ashes from his pipe, switched out the lights in his study, and went out into the hall. His foot was on the first stair when he heard a sound at the front door — a queer, scrabbling sound, like fingers clawing at the panels . . .

He turned quickly, staring through the darkness at the closed door. The scratching sound ceased and was replaced by a dull thudding, as though someone were beating with a clenched fist on the lower part of the door . . .

Colgate-Jones felt his way across the hall, pressed down the light switch, pulled back the bolts, and jerked the heavy door open. Something fell sprawling over the threshold into the dim pool of light from the shaded lamp — something that he saw, with a sudden catch of his breath, was the sodden figure of a man.

For an instant he thought the man was drunk, and then he saw that the water, which was running from his clothes and collecting in little shining puddles on the tiled floor, was streaked with red . . .

Colgate-Jones knelt down beside the stranger and raised his head.

'What's the matter?' he asked. 'Have you hurt yourself?'

The man coughed faintly and his closed eyes flickered open.

'They . . . they . . . ' He coughed again, choked, and was silent.

The puzzled clergyman stared down at him anxiously. His clothes were covered in mud and he was evidently badly hurt. Had he been knocked down by a car in the blackout? It was useless speculating. The thing to do was to get him inside and send for a doctor at once. The fellow looked as though he were dying . . .

Colgate-Jones picked him up under the arms and dragged him into the study. With difficulty he managed to lift him on to the settee. The man coughed again as he laid him down, but his eyes remained closed. It looked very much as though he were past speech. Thoroughly alarmed, Colgate-Jones hurried into the dining room, found a bottle of brandy, splashed some into a glass, and going back to the study, forced as much of the spirit as he could down the man's throat. It appeared to have very little effect, but it was all he could do for the moment. Going to the telephone he called the doctor's number. After some delay he was connected and heard Doctor Swinton's sleepy voice at the other end of the wire.

As concisely as possible he related what had happened.

'You'd better get here as quickly as you can,' he concluded. 'The man appears to me to be dying.'

The doctor grunted something which Colgate-Jones translated as a promise to come at once. With a sigh of relief he hung up the receiver and went back to the man on the settee. His eyes were still closed, but he was breathing very faintly. Bending down, the clergyman examined him more closely, and now, in the brighter light of the study lamp, he saw something which brought the breath hissing through his teeth. This was no motor accident. This was no accident of any sort. The narrow slit in the front of the shabby coat, around which the blood was spreading in an ever widening patch, was sufficient evidence of that.

Colgate-Jones felt a queer little tingle go pulsing through him. He remembered the faint cry which he had put down as the distant scream of a night bird. The man must have uttered it at the moment the murderous attack had evidently been made on him. The words which he had uttered with so much difficulty now took on a more sinister significance . . .

The closed lids quivered and the man on the settee opened his eyes. The pupils moved restlessly from side to side and he attempted to raise himself.

'Gently,' said Colgate-Jones soothingly, pushing him back against the cushions. 'You'd better keep still. You've been badly hurt. I've sent for a doctor . . . '

'I'm . . . done for.' The speech was slurred and nearly inaudible. 'Listen . . . listen . . . ' He stopped and his face twisted with pain, but with a desperate effort he went on even more weakly than before. 'X.1 . . . tell . . . twenty-first . . . find

8

X.1 . . . ' His breath was coming now in jerky gasps, whistling in his throat with a sound that was horrible in its significance. A tiny trickle of blood, vividly scarlet against the paper-white face, ran from the right corner of his mouth.

'Take it easy,' said the clergyman soothingly. 'Don't distress yourself . . . '

'X.1 . . . Dene . . . You must . . . ' His head fell back and his eyes closed. For a moment Colgate-Jones thought he had gone, but suddenly he rallied.

'Toothpaste . . . toothpaste . . . ' he muttered, struggling up on one elbow. 'The sig . . . '

He stopped, his voice breaking like the snapping of a thread, and fell back. This time there was no doubt. The man was dead!

The Reverend Colgate-Jones straightened up, took his handkerchief from his pocket, and wiped his damp face which was a shade less florid than usual. Into the quiet atmosphere of his study had come something terrible and violent — a fetid breath of all the filthy ugliness of war. There was no need to wonder what the dead man had been, or why he had died. The mention of Dene was sufficient to indicate his occupation. He had been a member of the British Intelligence Department — one of that small band of brave and unknown men who work in the dark without thought of fame, whose successes meet with little reward, and whose failures are more often than not punished by death. And he had evidently learned something — something of such vital importance that his death had been necessary to ensure his silence.

Colgate-Jones rubbed his smooth chin. Something ought to be done at once. The matter was obviously urgent. The proper authorities should be notified immediately. They would probably be able to make sense of the dead man's last words, which was certainly more than he could. He went to his desk and wrote down exactly what the dead man had said, while it was fresh in his memory, putting dots to denote the many pauses he had made. Then he picked up the telephone, glanced at a card hanging above the desk, and called a number. Michael Dene had told him once that that number would always find him. There was very little delay in getting through and, to his delight, it was Dene's voice which answered him.

'This is Colgate-Jones speaking,' said the clergyman. 'From the vicarage. Oh, I'm all right, thanks. Look here, Dene, a terrible thing has happened here tonight and it concerns you . . . ' He gave a hasty account of what had occurred. 'What shall I do?'

'Nothing,' answered Dene curtly. 'You don't know what a big thing this is, Jones. I know a little of what this fellow was talking about — a very little, I'm afraid, but enough to realize that it is of the very first importance. I'll come right along.'

'Had I better inform the police?' asked Colgate-Jones.

'No,' said Dene quickly. 'Do nothing until I get there. I should be with you in under two hours. Don't lose that paper with that fellow's last words. It's most important. Goodbye.'

He rang off, and as the vicar was putting the receiver back on its hook there was a little exclamation from the doorway.

'Oh,' said a voice — a very pleasant, slightly husky voice. 'It's you, is it? I heard somebody talking and wondered what was the matter. Why haven't you gone to bed? Has there been a raid warning?'

'No, no, my dear.' Colgate-Jones hastily stepped between the slim girl in the doorway and the dead man on the settee. 'There's been a little trouble — somebody has met with an accident. Run off back to bed, there's a good girl.'

Carol Wray pushed the fair hair back from her forehead, and drew the silken dressing-gown closer round her.

'Stop treating me as if I were still a child, Kupie,' she said, calmly coming farther into the room. 'I'm *not* going back to bed. I want to know what's going on.' She peered at the settee and caught her breath. 'Is that — is that the accident?' she whispered.

Colgate-Jones nodded.

'Is he — dead?' she asked.

'I'm afraid he is,' admitted her uncle. 'I really wish you would go back to your room, Carol . . . '

12

'Don't be silly,' she said impatiently. 'Who is it?'

'I don't know,' replied the clergyman, and she looked at him quickly, her blue eyes wide.

'You don't know?' she repeated in astonishment. 'How did he get here, then?'

Colgate-Jones told her. Just as he finished there was a knock at the front door.

'That'll be Doctor Swinton,' he said. 'You'll *have* to go now, Carol. You can't stop here while he makes his examination . . .'

'I'll make some coffee,' she replied, and ran swiftly away to the kitchen as he opened the front door.

'Come in, Swinton . . . ' he began, and then he saw that it was not Doctor Swinton who stood on the threshold. It was a much taller, altogether bigger man. Before he had time to recover from his surprise, the visitor stepped quickly into the hall, and Colgate-Jones found himself staring into the black muzzle of an automatic pistol.

'Keep still and do as you're told,'

snapped the newcomer. 'You will not be hurt if you do as you're told.'

'What do you want?' demanded the clergyman.

'A man came here a few minutes ago,' answered the visitor, 'a wounded man. I want *him*.'

'You are going to be unlucky,' said Colgate-Jones. 'A man came here, certainly — a dying man. He died . . . '

Suppressing his anger at the man's tone, the clergyman led the way into his study in silence. Still without a word he pointed to the figure on the settee. Warily the big man went to the body and gave it a quick glance.

'H'm, he's dead right enough,' he muttered, and there was relief in his voice. 'Did he speak before he died?'

'No,' said Colgate-Jones.

'You're sure?' The other eyed him searchingly. 'He said nothing — nothing at all?'

'Nothing at all,' declared the clergyman, returning his gaze steadily. At that precise moment every light in the room went out and it was plunged into total darkness.

2

Saturday — 2.30 a.m.

Some instinct warned Colgate-Jones to drop to the floor as the darkness came, and it was as well that he obeyed it. A streak of white flame leapt from the place where the intruder had been standing, and the explosion that followed was deafening. The bullet thudded into the wall somewhere near the fireplace, and then there came a sharp scream and a flood of foul language.

The wondering clergyman heard the man stamping about in the blackness, and then he screamed again and something fell to the floor. There was a crash in the hall, more foul language, and the banging of the front door.

Colgate-Jones, unable to make anything of this new development, listened, but everything was now quiet. Cautiously he began to scramble to his feet, and he had just succeeded when, as suddenly as they had gone out, the lights came on.

Blinking, he looked about him, and the first thing he saw was the automatic which the unknown man had carried lying on the floor near to where he had been standing.

'You'd better pick that up, Kupie,' said Carol's cool voice. 'If we have any more visitors like that one, it'll be useful.'

She came calmly into the room still clad in her dressing-gown and filmy crêpe pyjamas.

'Aren't you glad I didn't go back to bed?' she demanded.

Her uncle's jovial face broke into a smile.

'I suppose you put those lights out?' he said, and she nodded.

'I turned the main switch,' she answered. 'It was the only thing I could think of at that moment.'

'What happened after that?' he asked, his eyes twinkling. 'What made our friend scream and use such horrible language?'

'The meat fork!' she answered. 'I stuck it in his leg!'

She looked so demure as she said it that Colgate-Jones chuckled outright. And then he grew suddenly grave.

'It was a very dangerous thing to do,' he said seriously. 'If that brute had caught you . . .'

'I crawled in on the floor,' she interrupted. 'He did *try* to catch me, but he couldn't find me. I managed to get in another dig which must have caught him in the hand. Anyway, he dropped his pistol and ran. He's knocked over our coat-stand.'

'He has also planted a bullet in the wall,' remarked her uncle grimly. He picked up the pistol and examined it under the light.

'A German Mauser,' he muttered.

She was at his side, peering curiously at the weapon.

'A German pistol!' she exclaimed. 'Was he . . . ?'

'Yes, I think he was,' said Colgate-Jones.

'D'you think he killed — *him?*' asked Carol, looking quickly toward the settee.

'It seems more than probable,' replied

17

the clergyman. 'I . . . '

He stopped. For the second time that night there came a loud knock at the front door.

'That should be Swinton,' said Colgate-Jones, 'but I'm taking no chances this time.'

Gripping the automatic firmly he went out into the hall, and, stooping, called through the letter box:

'Is that you, Swinton?'

'Certainly it is,' answered a voice testily. 'What the devil are you playing at, Jones?'

'The devil has been pretty busy round here tonight, but he certainly hasn't been playing.' Colgate-Jones turned the handle as he spoke and pulled open the door. In out of the darkness came a man with a fierce grey moustache. His shrewd eyes were black and gimlety. They lit upon the pistol in the vicar's hand, and the bushy brows rose sharply.

'What the hell is going on here?' barked Doctor Swinton. 'Why are you marching about with that thing, eh?'

'A precaution, Swinton,' answered the clergyman. 'Don't stand in the doorway,

18

man. Come on in!'

'Have you gone cuckoo?' The doctor glared at him as he stepped into the hall. 'What's all this tomfoolery? Where's my patient?'

'Dead, I'm afraid,' retorted Colgate-Jones. 'Come into the study.'

Carol had disappeared. Apparently having assured herself that this time the visitor really was Doctor Swinton, she had gone back to the kitchen and her interrupted coffee-making.

Swinton threw his hat on a chair, deposited his bag on the floor, and strode over to the settee. For a second he stared down at the dead man with pursed lips, and then, without waste of either breath or time, he got busy.

At the end of five minutes, he looked round over his shoulder.

'This man was murdered. I suppose you know that?' he grunted.

'Yes, I know that,' said Colgate-Jones.

'How did it happen?' Swinton straightened up and came over to the other's side. The clergyman shook his bald head.

'I don't know,' he answered. 'I found

him on the doorstep, as I've already told you . . . '

'This is a police case, you know that?' broke in the doctor bluntly. 'Have you notified them?'

'No,' Colgate-Jones shook his head again. 'Neither am I going to — yet. Look here, can I rely on your discretion, Swinton?'

Swinton's gimlet eyes bored into him searchingly.

'You've known me long enough to make that remark superfluous,' he snapped.

'Yes, I think I have. But this is a big thing.' The vicar picked up a newspaper and gently spread it over the dead man's face. 'Listen, and I'll tell you.'

Swinton leaned back against the table, keeping his sharp eyes fixed unblinkingly on the other's face.

'Go on,' he said briefly. As the clergyman began, Carol came quietly in with the coffee, handed each a cup, and curled herself up on a footstool in front of the fire.

'H'm, incredible!' said the doctor when he had finished. 'Nazi agents in Claybury!

It sounds ridiculous.'

'I know, but it's true,' said Colgate-Jones.

'Can I stay and see this man, Dene?' asked Swinton.

'Do,' said the clergyman. 'I was hoping you would.'

'More coffee,' said Carol, and busied herself filling their empty cups.

Michael Dene arrived just before two. He was a tall man, lean and wiry, with grey eyes that looked infinitely weary. He shook hands warmly with Colgate-Jones, bowed to Carol and Swinton, and came almost immediately to the purpose of his visit.

'Tell me everything exactly as it happened,' he said, and Colgate-Jones complied. When he had finished, Dene went over to the settee, lifted the newspaper which covered the face of the dead man, gave a swift glance, and quietly let it drop back into place.

'Clavering,' he announced briefly. 'I thought it might be he. I had a note from him a few days ago saying he was on to something big. H'm,' he stroked his chin, and his face was very serious. 'It looks as though he were right,' he added softly.

'Do you understand what he meant by those words of his just before he died?' asked Colgate-Jones.

'Partly,' answered Dene. 'A very small part, though, I'm afraid.' He looked from one to the other — a searching look, as though he were weighing them up in his mind. 'This is a very serious matter,' he went on slowly after a long pause, 'and before going any further I must ask you all to promise me that nothing that is said, or that may transpire here tonight, will go beyond this room.'

'That's understood,' said the clergyman quickly, and the other two murmured an assent.

'It may strike you as rather a melodramatic request to make,' continued Dene, 'but, if you knew as much as I do — if you'd seen as much as I have during the last eighteen months — you'd understand. Anyway, this is an age of melodrama. Things are happening in the world today that make all the imaginings of the fiction-writer seem very milk and watery. We are facing a crisis more serious than any this country has ever faced before. We are fighting not only brawn but brains. Make no mistake about that. The German High Command is clever — clever and cunning. We have yet to realize just how cunning. You would imagine that we have had plenty of proof — the occupation of France without any other evidence should have been sufficient to make us realize this. But we are like mummies encased in tradition and red tape. What has happened to other countries could not possibly happen to us.' He gave a short, hard laugh. 'That belief is our greatest danger — that and our utter inability to realize the value of timing . . . ' He stopped abruptly. 'What's the use of going into all that,' he went on in a changed voice. 'There's lots to be done, and done at once. You and I, Jones, have worked together before. It looks as though we shall be working together again soon. Before this is through I may want your help.'

'You can count on it,' said Colgate-Jones quickly, and there was a gleam of sheer delight in his eyes.

'And mine, if I can be of any use,' said Carol.

'Thank you both,' said Dene. He pulled out a case and helped himself to a cigarette. 'I'll tell you all I know about this affair. It's mostly rumours that have filtered in from our agents, both here and abroad. Something is being planned — *has* been planned. Something big — something that would deal, or aim at dealing, a crippling blow at the nation — something that has been prepared long before an actual war had been declared — a plan that was all ready to be put into immediate execution *when the right moment came.* That is the lines on which the Nazis have always worked — a careful preliminary preparation and sudden surprise action.' He paused and took a long pull at his cigarette. 'As far back as the summer of nineteen thirty-six,' he went on, 'we suspected the preparation of some such scheme, and the Special Branch tried its utmost to discover what this plan was. We failed completely, but we did discover that there *was* such a plan and that it had been put in charge of X.1.'

'Who is X.1?' asked Colgate-Jones.

'X.1 is the cleverest of all the Nazi agents,' replied Michael Dene. 'Other than that I can't tell you. Nobody knows who X.1 is — not even his fellow agents in the German Intelligence Department. It is said in Berlin that only one person does know the real identity of X.1 and that person is Hitler himself.'

Colgate-Jones pursed his lips in a silent whistle that made him look even more cherubic than usual.

'So that's what Clavering was getting at, eh?' he muttered.

Michael Dene shot him a swift glance of appreciation.

'Your brain works quickly,' he said with a faint smile. 'According to how I read those disjointed words that Clavering uttered before he died, X.1 is going to give the signal to start this thing, whatever it is . . . '

'On the twenty-first?' interrupted the clergyman.

Dene nodded.

'On the twenty-first, Jones,' he said

gravely. 'The twenty-first of this month.'

'Why this month?' asked Colgate-Jones quickly.

Michael Dene eyed him thoughtfully.

'I can't tell even you that, Jones,' he said after a pause. 'Later, maybe, I shall have to, but I can't at the moment. There's a good reason why I think that whatever is going to happen is on the twenty-first of this month — a very good reason — but you'll have to take my word for it.'

Colgate-Jones stepped over to his desk and picked up a calendar.

'That's on a Saturday,' he said.

'Just eight days from now,' answered Michael Dene, and there was a worried wrinkle between his grey eyes. 'We've got to work fast, Jones. We've got to find X.1 before those eight days are up.'

'Do you know anything about him?' grunted Doctor Swinton.

'Nothing!' replied Dene. 'I couldn't even say that X.1 is a 'he'.'

'Do you mean that he — may be a woman?' said Carol.

'He might be anybody — I just don't

26

know,' declared Dene candidly.

'But — if you know nothing — nothing at all — how do you propose to find this person?' exclaimed the doctor. 'It's an impossible task . . . '

'It's got to be made possible!' snapped Dene. 'If those dying words of poor Clavering's mean anything — and the manner of his death, coupled with the man who came here tonight, prove that they do — X.1 has *got* to be found before the twenty-first!'

There was a silence. The rain lashed the window-panes violently. Somewhere outside an owl hooted mournfully, and from the river a wild duck broke suddenly into a sound that was so like a sardonic chuckle that Carol gave a little shiver.

Colgate-Jones broke the silence.

'What,' he said thoughtfully, 'did Clavering mean by his reference to 'toothpaste'?'

'God knows!' said Dene. He consulted the slip of paper on which the clergyman had scribbled the dying man's words. 'Have you got these down exactly as he uttered them?'

'Exactly,' said the vicar. 'I've put dots to represent the pauses he made.'

'Then it looks to me,' muttered Dene, frowning at the paper, 'as if 'toothpaste' had something to do with the signal which X.1 will give.'

He slipped off the side of the desk on which he had been sitting, and went over to the dead man.

'You didn't search his pockets, did you?' he asked over his shoulder.

'No,' answered Colgate-Jones. 'I didn't touch him more than was necessary.'

'Then there may be something,' muttered Dene. 'If these brutes hadn't time . . . ' He left the sentence unfinished, and began to go through Clavering's pockets. He brought to light a fair quantity of money, a cigarette-case, and a crumpled paper. Smoothing this out, he discovered that it was a menu card. Across the top was printed in flamboyant lettering: 'The Flaming Dawn.' He turned it over in the hope that the dead man might have used it to scribble some kind of notes, but there was nothing.

'Have you found something?' asked

Colgate-Jones, coming over to his side.

Dene shook his head.

'Nothing much,' he answered ruefully. 'Have you heard of a place called 'The Flaming Dawn'?'

'Yes,' broke in Carol instantly. 'It's a road-house near Staines — I've been there.'

'So had Clavering, apparently,' murmured Dene. 'A road-house near Staines, eh? I wonder . . . ?'

'It's the usual kind of place,' said the girl. 'The food's not bad and the band's passable. It was rather dull, I thought.'

'There's no date on this thing,' said Dene, 'but it doesn't look as though he had carried it about with him for long.' He looked at the clock. 'It's too late to go now, but I think tomorrow night we should pay a visit to 'The Flaming Dawn'. It might be profitable.'

3

Saturday — 4 a.m.

'I think it might,' agreed Carol with an approving nod. 'It was closed during the early days of the war, but it's been reopened now for two or three months. You know, there *is* a clue to X.1, or at any rate there's a clue that might *lead* you to X.1. I've thought so all along, and now you've found that menu, I'm sure.'

'What?' asked Michael Dene.

'Well, the fact that Mr. Clavering was killed near here is a clue, isn't it?' she answered. 'Something connected with this plot must be in this district, or *he* wouldn't have been here . . .'

Dene gave a quick exclamation.

'You're right, Miss Wray,' he cried. 'There *is* a clue there. I must have been blind not to have thought of it before. You get full marks for that.'

Carol made a face at Colgate-Jones.

'And you wanted to send me to bed!' she murmured reproachfully.

Doctor Swinton rose to his feet.

'I'm going to send myself to bed,' he grunted. 'I've got a heavy day tomorrow. If there's anything I can do to help, you've only to ask me . . .'

'I'm going, too,' said Dene, but the vicar interrupted him.

'Why not stay?' he suggested. 'There's plenty of room . . .'

'I'd like to, but I must go back,' said Dene. 'I'll see you again during the day, though. In the meanwhile, I'd better drop into the police-station and notify them about this. They'll have to be told. You won't have any trouble. I'll explain everything.'

He said good night to the girl, and Colgate-Jones accompanied both he and the doctor to the front door.

It was a pitch-black night except for the dim light on Dene's car, and the vicar came out on the step to see them off, closing the door behind him to prevent the light from showing.

'Well, good night, Dene,' he said.

'Come as early as you can . . . '

A gust of wind blew the door open behind him, and he was silhouetted against the light. As he turned to pull the door shut, there was a flash of light from the darkness of the garden, a sharp retort, and a bullet whined past his head and smacked into the woodwork of the porch with a vicious thud.

'Get inside!' snapped Dene. 'Get inside, Jones!'

But Colgate-Jones declined to do anything of the sort. He pulled the door to with a bang, blotting out the light against which he had offered such a good target for the hidden marksman, and hurrying down the steps, pressed himself against the wall at the side of the porch.

'The shot came from those trees over there,' whispered Dene. 'Stay where you are, I'm going to see if I can find who fired it.'

'I'd like to get my hands on him!' growled Swinton angrily. 'He nearly ruined my hat!'

'You stay with Jones,' muttered Dene. 'Too many cooks may very easily spoil the broth.'

He faded away in the darkness, moving as silently as a floating feather. In that dead blackout, with the rain hissing down around him to cover any slight noise he might make, it would be a clever sniper indeed who could pick him off. It was doubtful if he could be seen at all except at very close quarters, and it was a chance that he could not afford to miss. Somewhere under the dripping trees that flanked the vicarage lawn lurked the men who had been responsible for the death of Clavering, waiting to finish their night's work . . .

Dene pulled a pistol from his pocket as he crossed the sodden turf. At last he reached the trees and paused, listening. The branches rustled in the wind, and with every gust discharged a shower of raindrops that pattered round him, but apart from this there was no sound.

It was queerly eerie, standing there in the almost palpable darkness, unable to see more than a yard in any direction, and knowing that within a short distance an enemy waited. It was possible, of course, that after firing that single shot the hidden man, or men, had gone. But Dene did not think it was likely. They had come — he was convinced that there was more than one — for a purpose — to prevent Colgate-Jones, or anyone else, from passing on any information that Clavering might have divulged before he died, and that purpose had not been accomplished. They would not want to go back and report failure to the person who had sent them. Which meant that they would certainly make another attempt. That single shot had been a mistake in strategy. That a mass attack had been planned on the vicarage seemed certain, and the firing of that shot had given away the presence of the attackers. A faint movement somewhere to his left made Dene turn quickly, straining his eyes to try and see through the blackness. Suddenly there was a wailing scream that brought his heart into his mouth, and a beating of wings against wet leaves. He felt the rush of wind as something flew past his head, and realization came to him. An owl had been disturbed from its resting-place, that was all.

But something must have disturbed it. Dene stole forward, alert and watchful. In that dense blackness, this dangerous game of blind-man's-buff called for a concentration of all the senses. A slight sound within a yard or two brought him round sharply. Against the darkness a blacker shape had appeared from the shelter of one of the trees — a dark leaping shape that was already on him. Before he could bring his pistol up, something struck him on the head violently. Half-stunned, he reeled, stumbled, and fell to his knees, the automatic slipping out of his hand. A powerful grip on his throat contracted, and his mouth opened as his lungs were denied the air they craved. Somehow he managed to struggle to his feet although the grip still encircled his throat, and, with every effort he could muster, tried to free himself. But all the advantage was with the attacker. The blow which had caught him unaware had dazed him, and the man he was fighting was abnormally strong . . .

He felt his senses swimming under the pressure on his throat, and gathered himself for a final supreme effort to break away. His knee came up with a savage jerk into the pit of his assailant's stomach, and at the same instant he delivered a smashing uppercut to the unseen face. The man gave a grunt and a gasp, and the hold on his throat relaxed. Again he slammed home with his right, but this time the blow missed.

Dene staggered as a swinging left-hander crashed between his eyes, and felt a sudden surprise at the method of attack. He had expected to feel a knife tearing into his flesh, but, most astonishingly, the other had attacked with his bare fists.

A hand came groping for his throat again, but he gripped the sinewy wrist, and although he was almost spent, managed by a trick, that must have almost broken the other's arm, to fling him off. As he did so, he trod on something hard and guessed that it was his automatic.

Stooping swiftly, he snatched it up. As he straightened himself, a heavy blow on the jaw sent him rocking on his heels. But the pistol was in his hand now, and when his unseen antagonist came leaping at him again, Dene rammed the muzzle into his side.

The man recognized the force of that argument at once. He became suddenly motionless, and Dene made full use of his advantage.

'Keep still, or I'll blow a hole through you!' he muttered breathlessly. 'I mean that!'

He fumbled in his pocket with his free hand and pulled out a torch. Pressing the button he directed a white ray into the face of his captive. And then he gasped in astonishment.

'You!' he said.

The face of the man blinking in the sudden glare was the face of one of his own men — E.9 of the British Intelligence Department.

4

Except for the map which entirely covered the top of a large table, the room was ordinary. So were the two men who sat before the fire in the solidly comfortable easy-chairs. The house, of which the room formed a part, was ordinary: one of many occupying a very ordinary housing-estate similar to all other housing-estates that had ever been designed.

The owner of the house, a fat, red-faced man, with small twinkling blue eyes and a perpetual smile, was ordinary, too. His name, Horace Smith, was not only ordinary but commonplace.

There were only two things that were not at all ordinary. The very large map of the British Isles, with its seven different coloured sections, and the conversation of the two men who sat before the dying fire.

'Hanson should be back by now, Jenkins,' remarked Mr. Horace Smith, who was known to the Third Reich as Y.3, breaking a long silence.

His friend, a thin, gloomy man, nodded and carefully deposited a cone of ash from his cigar in the tray at his elbow.

'I hope,' continued Mr. Smith thoughtfully. 'I hope there has been no trouble.'

'Hanson's not alone,' grunted the gloomy Mr. Jenkins, who was known to the Third Reich as Y.4.

'The time for which we have all been working is nearly at hand,' murmured Mr. Smith, smiling benignly at the other. 'It would be a pity if anything went wrong now.'

'I don't see why anything should go wrong,' replied the taciturn Mr. Jenkins. 'That fellow, Clavering, stumbled on his knowledge by sheer accident. He's no longer in a position to use it. What are you worrying about?'

'My dear fellow, I'm not worrying,' declared Mr. Smith, shaking his head gently. 'A little anxious perhaps, but not worrying.'

Nothing could have been more typical of the average, fairly prosperous, suburban business man than these two. Their surroundings, their appearance, their tone of voice — all were essentially English. Their very names stamped them. And yet in the veins of each ran German blood.

It has been said by an expert who understands such things that the way to play a part successfully is to *be* it; to soak oneself so thoroughly in the atmosphere of the role it is desired to portray that it eventually becomes second nature; to study every little mannerism consistent with that character, to practise them assiduously, and to even think in the way which that particular person would think. Herein lay the secret of these men's immunity from suspicion for a long period of years, and herein, also, was the secret of the men who worked with them.

They not only appeared to *be* what they looked — they *were*.

Everything they did was consistent, hence nobody had the slightest idea that they were other than they seemed.

After a little while Mr. Smith rose, and

going over to the table peered down at the map. In the various coloured sections were innumerable little circles drawn in red. They covered the entire map like the outbreak of an ugly skin disease.

'It will be a devastating blow,' murmured Mr. Smith, with his placid, benevolent smile. 'A devastating blow. What a useful person the fanatic is, Jenkins.'

Mr. Jenkins achieved a queer sound that was evidently his way of laughing.

'These people with grievances,' continued the fat man, shaking his head. 'If they only knew how often they were *used* by more intelligent men, eh?'

'They've certainly been very useful in this instance,' said Mr. Jenkins.

'And they don't know it,' chuckled Mr. Smith. 'They don't know it.'

Still chuckling, he picked up the real table-top, which stood against the wall, placed it carefully in position over the map, and adjusted two screws which held it firmly.

'The twenty-first,' he said, coming back to his chair. 'The twenty-first will give these stupid, complacent English a rude awakening. Such a thing would be *impossible* in Germany.'

'The English people are too easy-going,' grunted Mr. Jenkins. 'They are allowed too much latitude — to say and do too much as they like. They are allowed to think too much for themselves.'

'When they have been absorbed by the Third Reich,' remarked Mr. Smith, 'it will be different. Our Gestapo will see to that. There is Hanson now, I think.'

The door opened, and the man who had held up Colgate-Jones a short while before came in. He was limping and about his right hand had been tied a handkerchief. He was followed by two other men, a small man, broad of shoulder and stockily built, and a thin, lean man, not unlike the gloomy Mr. Jenkins in appearance.

'Well?' queried Mr. Smith, smiling genially.

'It is far from well,' answered Hanson. 'We shall have to do something, and quickly.'

The smile vanished from the fat man's face.

'What has happened?' he demanded sharply.

Hanson walked over to the sideboard and poured himself out a large Johnnie Walker which he gulped neat.

'Dene is here,' he said, setting down the empty glass so roughly that it cracked.

'Dene!' echoed Mr. Smith. 'Michael Dene?'

Hanson nodded.

'They know something,' he said harshly. 'Clavering must have spoken before he died.'

'But I thought you . . . ' began Jenkins.

'I did,' snapped Hanson. 'I'll tell you what happened . . . '

He gave an account of his interview with Colgate-Jones, and the sequel.

'I don't know who it was who stabbed me in the leg and hand,' he concluded, 'but when I do, I'll make them suffer for it.'

'But how do you know Dene's here?' demanded Mr. Smith quickly.

'I saw him arrive,' was the reply. 'After I left the vicarage I rejoined Altman and

Trigford in the car. We left it in a field, and all three of us went back to the house. I was suspicious of that parson. He said Clavering hadn't spoken, but I didn't believe him. He's not used to lying, and he didn't do it well. I wanted to see what was going to happen. The natural thing for him to do was to send for the police, but he didn't. If he had I should have seen them arrive. Only the doctor arrived at first, and then, after a long interval, another car. I saw the man who came in that as he was let into the house — saw him clearly for a second in the light from the hall. It was Dene!'

'Then this man, Colgate-Jones, must have telephoned him,' muttered Mr. Smith. 'And if he telephoned him it must be because Clavering said something before he died.'

'That's what I think,' agreed Hanson.

'There's another thing,' put in Jenkins. 'If Colgate-Jones telephoned Dene, he must know him . . . '

'You're right,' interrupted Mr. Smith, and he was no longer looking placid and genial. The twinkling blue eyes had hardened, and there was a set expression about the small, over-red mouth that was ugly. 'We must do something at once. If Clavering managed to pass anything on to Jones, and he has told Dene, we must stop it going any farther. It wants several hours to dawn and the vicarage is not far away. We have time . . . '

'Wait,' said Hanson. 'Dene is leaving. I saw him starting and tried to shoot him, but I missed. He will have gone by the time we get there . . . '

'It doesn't matter,' snapped Mr. Smith impatiently. 'Dene can be dealt with later. Colgate-Jones is of equal importance. *He* will be there.'

'X.1 should be told about this, don't you think?' suggested Jenkins.

'I will send a message to the usual place,' answered Mr. Smith. 'Now go after Colgate-Jones. There are four of you, it should be easy.'

'What are you going to do?' asked Hanson.

'I cannot join you,' said Mr. Smith, who was known to the Third Reich as Y.3. 'I am due for A.R.P. duty in a few minutes' time.'

5

Saturday — 5 a.m.

'Stacey!' exclaimed Michael Dene, when he had recovered sufficiently from his surprise to be able to speak at all.

'Good God, it's the Chief!' cried his captive. 'Talk about dog eating dog!' He rubbed his arm ruefully. 'Would you mind taking that gun out of my ribs, sir?'

Dene removed the weapon and thrust it into his pocket.

'What are you doing here?' he demanded.

'I had a note from Clavering asking me to meet him here,' answered Stacey.

'To meet him — here?' repeated Dene.

'Well, not exactly on this spot, but near enough,' was the reply. 'To be exact, he asked me to meet him outside the church, which is just across the road. He never turned up, but that may be because I was late. I ran into a ditch in this damned blackout and busted the car. Luckily, I

46

wasn't very far away and I walked the rest of the distance . . . '

'I rather think that accident of yours cost Clavering his life,' broke in Dene gravely.

Out of the darkness, for as soon as he had made sure of the other's identity Dene had switched out his torch, came a gasp.

'Good Lord, sir! You don't mean that Clavering is dead?'

'Clavering was stabbed to death somewhere near here a few hours ago,' answered Dene. 'I've no doubt, now, that he was stabbed while he was waiting for you.'

He told Stacey what had happened, and the Secret Service man gave a low, hissing whistle.

'Was the man who stabbed him the man who fired that shot?' he asked.

'Did you see him?' asked Dene quickly.

'No,' Stacey shook his head, 'but I heard him. That's what brought me in here. I thought you were he . . . '

Dene uttered a short, mirthless laugh.

'I thought the same about you,' he said.

'Apparently we were both at cross purposes. While we were fighting, I suppose the man escaped.'

'There was more than one, I think, sir,' said Stacey. 'Phew! Fancy a bunch of Nazis in an English village, and at the vicarage of all places . . . '

'There's no fancy about it,' broke in Michael Dene grimly. 'You'd better come back to the house. I rather think, now you're here, you're going to be useful.'

He led the way across the lawn and presently rejoined Colgate-Jones and the doctor. The fight had been so silent that neither of them had heard anything of it.

Colgate-Jones chuckled when Dene explained.

'You'd better come in and have a wash and a drink,' he said. 'I dare say Mr. Stacey could do with one, too.'

'I certainly could!' declared Stacey fervently.

'Well, I'll be going,' grunted Swinton. 'Otherwise I shan't get any sleep at all. God help any Nazi thugs who try to stop me.'

They heard him drive away as they entered the hall.

'How long have you known Swinton?'

48

asked Dene. 'Trustworthy?'

'Quite.'

'You're sure?'

Colgate-Jones raised his eyebrows.

'As sure as any one man can be of another,' he replied. 'He's very well liked in the district in spite of his rather gruff manner. Perhaps because of it. He's a very good doctor.'

Michael Dene nodded and abruptly changed the subject.

'Look here, if I can use your telephone,' he said, 'I think I'll change my mind and stop.'

'Of course,' said the vicar. 'Will you put through your call now or have a wash first?' He looked critically at Dene's battered face and muddy clothes. 'I think if I may say so,' he murmured with a twinkle in his eyes, 'that unless your call is very urgent, I should have a wash first.'

Dene inspected himself in the hall mirror.

'That is very sound advice,' he remarked.

Both he and Stacey felt better after a wash, and even better still when they had consumed the drinks which Colgate-Jones had waiting for them in the dining room.

'Now I'll get my call through,' remarked Dene, setting down his empty glass, 'and then we can have another drink and a discussion.'

He left the vicar chatting to Stacey in the dining room and made his way to the study. After a short interval he came back.

'I shall have to forgo my call,' he announced seriously. 'The line is dead.'

'It was all right earlier,' said Colgate-Jones, and Dene nodded.

'I've no doubt it was,' he said. 'But since then somebody has very thoughtfully cut the wire.'

The clergyman looked at him steadily.

'It sounds like trouble,' he murmured.

Dene nodded slowly.

'I think something is due to happen,' he said. 'These people are going to try and make sure that if Clavering said anything before he died, it will go no farther.'

'What do you think they'll do?' asked Colgate-Jones.

Dene shrugged his shoulders.

'Some form of an attack on the house,'

he answered. 'It's obvious that something of the sort had been planned or the telephone wire wouldn't have been cut. I think we had better make certain that all the windows and doors are fastened. It will at least prevent a surprise.'

They made a hurried round of the ground floor. The vicarage was an old house, and most of the windows were provided with wooden shutters which, to help with the blackout regulations, the vicar had ordered should be closed at dusk.

'They won't find it so easy to get in,' said Dene, when they returned to the dining room. 'Where's Miss Wray?'

'She went up to her bedroom to dress,' replied Colgate-Jones.

'You'd better go up and tell her to stop there,' said Dene. 'If there is any trouble she'll be safer there.'

The clergyman nodded and hurried away. They heard him go up the stairs and knock on a door somewhere above.

'Supposing these chaps *don't* try to get in,' said Stacey thoughtfully.

Michael Dene looked up from the

automatic which he had taken from his pocket and was examining.

'What do you mean?' he asked.

'Well, wouldn't it be easier for them to blow the place up from the outside or something like that?' suggested the other.

'It would be easier,' answered Dene, 'but I doubt if they will attempt anything of the sort. An explosion would lead to an inquiry into the cause, and they don't want a lot of publicity.'

'Doesn't that apply to anything they may do?' said Stacey.

'In a way, but not quite in the same way,' replied Dene, slipping the pistol back in his pocket. 'For instance, if we were all found shot and the scene carefully arranged, it might be made to look like the work of burglars. There would be an inquiry, but it would take a different direction. See what I mean?'

Stacey nodded slowly.

'If this bunch is working somewhere in the neighbourhood, which I believe,' Dene went on, 'they don't want a floodlight turned on the place. It would be most embarrassing. No, whatever they do will be less spectacular than bombs or anything of that sort . . . '

He stopped as Colgate-Jones returned followed by Carol. The girl had changed into a neatly tailored suit of some dark material that accentuated the slim lines of her figure and her bright, honey-coloured hair.

'She won't stop upstairs,' said the clergyman helplessly.

'Of course not,' she said calmly, as though the suggestion was not even worth consideration. 'If there's anything happening, I'm going to be in it.'

'Something will certainly happen,' said Dene a little grimly, 'and it may be very unpleasant. I really think it would be better if you . . . '

'I know,' she interrupted, 'I've already been over all that with Kupie. He doesn't like me calling him that, but he *is* rather like one of those little celluloid dolls, isn't he? If he wore a broad band of blue silk ribbon round his tummy . . . '

'Really, Carol,' began Colgate-Jones, and Michael Dene laughed.

'There certainly *is* a resemblance,' he

said, and the vicar snorted indignantly.

'Well then, now I've joined the party,' continued Carol, perching herself on the arm of an easy-chair, and displaying quite a lot of very attractive silk-clad leg in the process, 'what do we do next?'

'We just wait,' replied Dene. 'I don't think we shall have to wait very long. Whatever is going to happen will happen soon. It'll be daylight shortly, and if we can keep these people off until then, we'll be safe — for the time being at least. They daren't come out into the open . . . '

He broke off abruptly to listen. The faintest of faint sounds had come from the hall, and with a gesture to the others to keep quiet, he went noiselessly to the door. The dim light from the centre pendant left much of the hall in darkness, and the sound — a gentle scratching — came from the shadows by the front entrance.

Dene moved softly across the polished floor until he was barely a foot from the door. There was somebody outside on the step, he could hear them plainly. The scratching sound continued, and he was puzzled to account for it. What were they up to? They were doing something to the door, but what?

His eyes roved over the inner surface of the heavy portal, but he could see nothing. The scratching sound went on, however, and he located it after a moment or two as coming from somewhere near the lock. Quite suddenly a little splinter of wood broke away, and he caught a glimpse of the end of a steel drill. It revolved rapidly for a second and was then withdrawn, leaving a hole about half an inch in diameter through the wood-work of the door.

He stepped quickly to one side and fingered the pistol in his pocket. The intention was obvious. They were going to drill round the lock until it was weak enough to be pushed out.

He glanced up at the two big bolts at the top and bottom of the door which he had shot during his tour of inspection a few minutes earlier, and his lips curled in a smile.

Even if they succeeded in cutting the lock, those bolts would hold the door for a long time. And then it occurred to him that *surely* they would be prepared for such a contingency. There were bolts on nearly every front door, and the men outside must have realized this.

His brows drew together. If they *had* realized it, then they must have also realized that this attack on the lock was useless. Why waste time here, the least vulnerable point, when there were other and easier ways of gaining access to the house?

The answer came to him almost before his mind had formed the question. This attack on the door was a blind. They had no intention of getting in that way at all. It was intended to distract attention while the real attack was concentrated at another point entirely.

Resisting an impulse to shoot through the hole in the hope of wounding the man with the drill, Dene slipped back to the study. In a low voice he acquainted the others with his discovery, and the conclusion he had drawn.

'It's almost certain,' he ended, 'that some of them are round at the back now. We'd

56

better form a kind of patrol, so that we can keep an eye on all the likely spots at which they may make an attempt to get in.'

'How many do you think there are outside?' asked Carol, her forehead wrinkled in a frown.

Dene shrugged his shoulders.

'I haven't the least idea,' he declared. 'There may be only a few, or they may have arrived in force. You've got that Mauser, haven't you, Jones?'

The vicar nodded, and produced the pistol from his pocket.

'What about you, Stacey?' Dene turned swiftly to the younger man. 'Are you armed?'

Stacey shook his head.

''Fraid I'm not,' he said ruefully.

'Then we've only got two weapons among us,' said Dene. 'Oh well, we shall have to make the best of those. Give your gun to Stacey, Jones. He's more used to handling a pistol than you are.'

Rather reluctantly Colgate-Jones complied. There was a gleam in his eyes that suggested that he would welcome a chance to use it himself.

'You slip through to the back, Stacey,' ordered Dene, 'and if you see anything, yell.' Stacey gave a brief nod and went out. 'You'd better stay here, Miss Wray,' continued Dene rapidly, 'and yell, too, if you hear anyone at the window. You keep an eye on the hall door, Jones, in case I've been wrong. I'll open the doors of the other rooms and watch them. We've got to keep these men from getting in — if they once do that I don't think we shall stand a hope in hell!'

He disappeared along the passage from which the other rooms opened. Inside the vicarage it was very still; outside the wind still sighed mournfully round the house. The rain appeared to have ceased: the patter of it was no longer audible. Dene peered into the darkened lounge and listened, but there was no sound. He did the same with the dining room — no sound here, either. He glanced at the illuminated dial of his wristwatch. Five-thirty. In a short while it would be getting light. The attack, if it came at all, would have to be soon . . .

It came at the moment, and from three

separate sources at once. There was a yell from Stacey, a splintering crash and the tinkle of breaking glass from the dining room, and a similar crash from the study.

Michael Dene made a rush for the dining room door, felt a cold draught of wind blowing out on him, and saw dimly the figure of a man at the window. He fired twice, and two answering bullets flew past his head and buried themselves in the wall of the passage behind him. A muffled shot from the direction of the kitchen warned him that Stacey was also dealing with an intruder. There was another crash of breaking glass from the study, and Colgate-Jones called frantically. Dene pulled the dining room door to with a bang, and twisted the key in the lock. That would hold up the intruder there for a minute or two while he went to the assistance of the vicar.

He found Colgate-Jones in the doorway of the study, and pulled him back just as a man who was climbing in through the shattered window raised his hand and fired. The shot crashed into the door-frame within an inch of the clergyman's head, and Dene retaliated with two shots in quick succession, one of which must have found a billet, for the man at the window gave a sharp cry of pain.

And then came an unexpected interruption from outside. There was the sound of confused shouting and a voice crying faintly: 'Spread your men out, Inspector. This way, come on!'

'It's all right, sir, we've got 'em!' answered a gruff voice, and the man at the window uttered an oath and slid out of sight. They heard him shout a warning to his companions, and there was a squelching scurry of running feet on wet gravel, and then a sudden silence.

'They've bolted,' muttered Michael Dene. 'The arrival of the police scared 'em . . . '

'How did the police get here?' grunted Colgate-Jones, wiping his face with a handkerchief.

'God knows,' answered Dene, 'but they were just in time. I don't think we could have held those brutes back for long.' He looked round the study. 'Where's Miss Wray?' he asked.

'She went upstairs,' answered the vicar. 'I . . . '

A golden head appeared at the broken window, and to their utter surprise Carol climbed gingerly into the room. Her clothes were awry and she was smeared with mud from head to foot.

'What — what on earth are you doing out there?' gasped Colgate-Jones. 'I thought you were upstairs . . . '

'I went upstairs,' she said calmly, 'but it's very easy to get out of the bathroom window on to the roof of that shed and then drop to the ground.'

'But — but what did you do it for?' demanded the vicar. 'My dear girl, it was a most *dangerous* thing to do . . . '

'I wanted to try my police act,' she answered. 'I thought it might work, and it did!'

'Your police act?' repeated Colgate-Jones, staring at her. 'That wasn't you?'

'Alone I did it!' she said. 'With the aid of a portable gramophone and the record of a dramatic sketch which I suddenly remembered I'd got. How did it sound?'

'Tremendous!' exclaimed Dene, and his

eyes were twinkling. 'It was a remarkable success. You're really a remarkable girl.'

She smiled mischievously.

'I'm quite useful to have about the house,' she said.

6

Saturday — 8.30 p.m.

Perhaps the most original thing about 'The Flaming Dawn' was its decorative scheme. Certainly in all other respects, so far as was outwardly visible, at any rate, it differed not at all from any other establishment of its kind.

There was the same microscopic dance floor, surrounded by tables and chairs; the same band perched on a raised dais at one end of the oblong room, playing the same tunes; the same weary looking waiters, hobbling painfully from table to table with an air of bored disgust at the entire proceedings; the same dance hostesses trying to conceal an infinite weariness behind a mask of unnatural gaiety that failed to brighten their tired eyes; and the same habitués shuffling about on the dance floor, or sitting talking at the various tables.

It is a curious fact that the people who make a habit of patronizing such places as 'The Flaming Dawn' seem to acquire a standard expression which makes them appear to have all been turned out of one mould.

When Michael Dene, Carol, Colgate-Jones, and Frank Stacey arrived the place was more than half empty, it being the comparative early hour of eight-thirty. The difficulty of getting in had been overcome by Stacey, who had been there before and was therefore able to sign in the rest of the party.

The band was playing a popular fox-trot as a deferential but slightly contemptuous-looking waiter conducted them to a table, and hovered over them expectantly.

Stacey consulted the others and gave an order, which the waiter shuffled away to execute.

It is a ponderable fact that while the law regards the consumption of a single whisky and soda, in such places, as a serious crime and severely punishable as such, it allows the consumption of an entire bottle with impunity, thus bearing out Mr. Bumble's classic description.

Colgate-Jones, who had discarded his clerical collar for the occasion, and arrayed himself in the conventional dinner-jacket, looked about him with interest.

'I'm not sure whether I like the mural decorations or not,' he murmured.

'Not, I'm sure,' said Carol. 'The effect is rather like badly fried eggs on rashers of impossible bacon!'

Michael Dene laughed. The description was not inapt.

In conformity with the name of the establishment, its proprietor had endeavoured to achieve an effect of sunrise. The sun rose everywhere. The band played before a rising sun; there were rising suns on the walls, and in odd alcoves; a tremendous rising sun in the form of a huge lampshade occupied the centre of the roof, and numerous other rising suns provided additional lighting. It was just a little overpowering.

'Have you often been here before?' asked Dene, looking across at Stacey.

He shook his head.

'About half a dozen times,' he replied. 'I came here once with poor Clavering.'

'Did he come here a lot?' said Dene quickly.

'A good bit, I think,' answered Stacey. 'There was a girl he knew ... ' He glanced quickly round and shook his head. 'She's not here tonight. He introduced me to her once — rather a nice girl, I thought she was.'

'Did he say anything in that note to you — except to make the appointment?' asked Dene, and for the third time Stacey shook his head.

'Nothing,' he said.

Dene frowned, and resting his elbow on the table, gently pinched his lower lip between a finger and thumb.

'This is going to be a devilishly difficult job,' he muttered. 'What did he find out, and how? What *is* going to happen on the twenty-first?' He looked from one to the other with troubled eyes. 'There's so much to be done and so little time to do it. We may be wasting our time here for all I know, and there's no time to waste.'

'Whatever it was that Clavering found out, it was pretty serious,' murmured Stacey. 'We've had proof of that. They wouldn't have made two attempts to shut us up if it wasn't.'

'It's serious enough,' said Michael Dene in a low voice. 'If it wasn't X.1 wouldn't be in it.' He struck his fist impatiently on the table. 'If only he'd had time to say more,' he breathed, 'just a *little* more.'

'It's almost a miracle that he was able to say as much as he did,' said Colgate-Jones softly. 'It must have been sheer willpower that kept him alive long enough.'

Dene gave him a warning glance as the waiter approached and set a bottle of whisky, glasses, and a siphon of soda water in front of them. They remained silent until he had gone again, and then it was Carol who spoke first.

'According to what Mr. Clavering said,' she murmured, 'X.1 is to give the signal to put this plan, whatever it is, into execution, isn't that right?'

Dene nodded.

'On the twenty-first,' he answered.

'Well, it seems to me that if you can find out *how* this signal is to be given, you'll also find X.1,' she said.

'That's fairly sound logic, Miss Wray,' agreed Dene, 'but how are we going to find out how this signal is to be given?'

'Toothpaste,' she answered. 'Toothpaste has got something to do with the giving of the signal. Plenty of soda for me, Mr. Stacey, please.'

Frank Stacey, who was pouring out the drinks, almost filled her glass and pushed it across the table toward her.

'Don't you think it's likely,' put in the Reverend Colgate-Jones, 'that now they know we are in possession of some knowledge concerning this conspiracy they'll change their plans?'

'No,' answered Dene instantly. 'If this thing is as big as I think it is, they won't be *able* to. They'll have gone too far with it to make any alterations. Besides, they don't know *how* much we know, although they probably guess that Clavering couldn't have had time to tell us much. Their attempts to get *us* out of the way have been more in the nature of a precaution than because they think we know too much. It's what we *might* find out that's worrying them, not what we *know*. And then you've got to take into consideration the German mentality. They love making plans, and they hate altering them. No, I think we can take it that the original scheme will go through — *unless* we can stop it in time.'

Carol took a cigarette-case out of her bag and helped herself to a cigarette.

'Have you any idea what form it's likely to take?' she asked.

'No.' Dene flicked open a lighter and leaning forward offered her a light. 'I wish I had, it would be easier. I can only conjecture several things it *might* be. It might be the spreading of an epidemic disease, or the release of quantities of poison-gas, or some form of tampering with the foodstuffs of the country, or the water supply . . . '

'But surely anything of the sort would be impossible,' protested Colgate-Jones. 'Either of the suggestions that you have

69

mentioned would necessitate a tremendous organization, involving hundreds of people . . . '

'Well, why not?' interrupted Dene. 'This wasn't planned yesterday, or the day before. This has been in preparation for years — ready to be put into action when the right moment came.'

'Do you mean that there are hundreds of Nazi agents in England?' said the girl with astonished eyes.

Dene smiled and shook his head.

'No,' he replied. 'There are several, a lot more than you would think, who have been here ever since the formation of the Third Reich, ordinary-looking people that no one would ever suspect. *They* are the organizers, and there are plenty of people to carry out their schemes, believe me. In every town throughout the country, you'll find a group of fanatics, devoted to some cause or other, men and women who are quite prepared to sacrifice their lives, if necessary. It's through *these* people that the Nazi agents work. They may never appear openly in the matter at all, but the orders come from them.' He leaned back in his chair and looked round. 'The place seems to be filling up a bit,' he said.

It was. By ones and twos and in little parties, people were trickling slowly into the oblong room, and taking their places at the tables round the dancing-floor. There was a good sprinkling of uniforms and a great display of bare shoulders. The chatter of voices was broken, every now and again, by a rippling laugh or a deep guffaw, and everybody seemed to be making frantic efforts to assure themselves, and each other, that they were having a good time.

Michael Dene wondered, as he let his eyes rove slowly from table to table, whether there was anyone else here on such a strange errand as he.

'Who runs this place, do you know?' he murmured to Stacey.

'A man named Pellissi,' answered the other. 'He's half Italian, half Greek, I believe.'

'A good mixture,' said Dene cynically, and returned to his lazy inspection of the room.

A small party, consisting of a man and

two women, had come in and were threading their way between the tables behind an obsequious waiter. The man was tall and grey-haired; the women young and pretty. One of them, a slim, dark-haired girl, was lovely.

Stacey touched him on the arm and he turned.

'You see that girl who has just come in — the dark one?' whispered Stacey. 'That was Clavering's girl.'

'Oh, was it?' Michael Dene became suddenly interested. 'You know her, don't you?'

'Only slightly,' answered Stacey. 'Her name's Janice Gould.'

'Only slightly will be enough,' said Dene. 'I want to meet her, Stacey. Choose a good moment and go over and introduce yourself. If you met her with Clavering she'll probably remember you. Bring her over here, if you can.' He looked at the girl, who was laughing at some remark which the grey-haired man had made. 'She might know something. Who are the people with her?'

Stacey shook his head.

'I don't know,' he replied.

The band started a waltz, and Dene looked across at Carol with one eyebrow upraised interrogatively.

'Care to dance?' he said.

Her eyes sparkled, and slipping off her cloak, she stood up.

'I suppose there's some deep design behind this apparently innocent invitation to the waltz?' she said, laughing up at him as he led her out on to the floor.

'You're far too quick on the uptake,' he answered. 'There *is* a design, though it's not very deep. I merely want to have a good look at the layout of this place, and this seems a good method of doing it.'

He was a good dancer and guided her skilfully between the couples crowding the tiny floor. As he came by the table where Janice Gould sat, he saw that she was now alone. The grey-haired man was dancing with the other girl. Stacey had, apparently, also noticed this fact, for when Dene glanced over to their table he saw that he had risen, and was starting to make his way over to her. When next he came round, Stacey was talking to her.

73

The waltz finished and there was a smattering of applause. Carol glanced up at him inquiringly.

'Not just now,' he murmured. 'I'm rather hoping that Stacey will bring that girl over to us. Do you mind?'

'Business before pleasure,' she replied. 'I enjoyed that. You really dance very nicely.'

'Thank you,' he said, and they made their way back to Colgate-Jones.

The vicar was bubbling over with suppressed excitement.

'We're being watched!' he said in a low voice. 'Don't look round, but there's a man at the table just to our left. He came in with another man from that little door by the band. The other man's gone now, but they were holding a whispered conversation about us.'

'How do you know?' demanded Dene quickly.

'I was watching 'em,' answered Colgate-Jones. 'In that!' He turned his eyes toward Carol's silver cigarette-case which was propped up against her evening bag on the table. 'I fixed it so that I could see 'em. It struck me as queer that they should have come from that door instead of by the usual entrance.'

'But how do you know they're watching us?' asked Dene.

'Because they kept looking over here, and at you and Carol while they were whispering together,' explained the clergyman triumphantly. 'They're watching us without a doubt.'

Michael Dene drew a cigarette-case from his pocket, handed it to the girl and to Colgate-Jones, and was helping himself when it slipped from his fingers and fell to the floor. Stooping to pick it up, he managed to get a glimpse of the man the vicar had mentioned. He was sitting by himself at a small table near the wall, staring rather gloomily at a whisky and soda, round the glass of which his fingers were loosely clasped. He did not appear to be taking much notice of anything or anybody.

Dene straightened up with a murmured word of apology to his companions, and lighted a cigarette.

'Queer looking bloke,' he said, trickling

a thin stream of smoke between his lips. 'I seem to have seen him somewhere before. Hello, Stacey's bringing the girl over.'

The grey-haired man was still dancing with the other girl, and Stacey had taken advantage of this to persuade Janice Gould to join them for a few minutes. This he explained when he introduced her.

There was something very fresh and likeable about Janice Gould. Dene took to her at once. She refused a drink, and they began chatting about various commonplace subjects.

During the conversation, Dene happened to glance casually round and caught a glimpse of the man at the table by the wall. He was staring fixedly at the dark-haired girl, and there was a look of consternation and a trace of fear on his red, unpleasant face. Catching Dene's eye, he looked quickly away, but the Secret Service man had seen enough to convince him that Colgate-Jones had been right. There was very little doubt that the man was one of the Nazi group, or at any rate connected with them.

'I rather expected Jim — Mr. Clavering tonight,' said Janice, breaking a short silence. 'Perhaps he'll come later; he said he would look in if he could.'

Carol gave Dene a quick glance, and the vicar fingered his glass nervously. Stacey shifted uneasily, and tried to cover his embarrassment by fumbling with his cigarette-case.

The girl sensed that something was wrong, and a little puzzled frown appeared on her face. She turned her large grey eyes from one to the other questioningly.

'What's the matter?' she began. 'Have I . . . ?'

Michael Dene leaned suddenly forward.

'Miss Gould,' he said, and his voice was deliberately void of any kind of emotion. 'There's something you ought to know. You've *got* to know sooner or later, and it might as well be now. But you've got to steel yourself, you understand? You must exhibit no sort of emotion whatever when you hear what I'm going to tell you. The fate of a good many people may depend on that — perhaps the fate of the whole country.'

She looked at him steadily.

'Is it about — about Jim?' she asked in a low voice.

He nodded.

'Tell me,' she whispered. 'I promise I won't make a scene or anything. Is he — has anything happened to him?'

'Why should you think that?' said Dene quickly.

'Because he told me — something might,' she answered.

'He was right,' said Dene softly. 'Remember your promise, Miss Gould — Jim Clavering won't come here any more.'

'I see.' She nodded slowly. 'I see. Will you make that drink you offered me just now a very large one, please.'

7

Dene poured out a generous portion of whisky and pushed it across the table.

'Drink it neat,' he ordered. 'It will do you more good.'

She nodded. Her face was quite devoid of expression as she lifted the glass slowly to her lips. Only the little pulse that beat in her throat gave evidence of any sort of emotion — that and the very faint twitching of her mouth.

There was a sudden drum-roll from the band dais and a stout, dark man stepped toward the microphone.

'Ladies and gentlemen,' he announced in a slightly nasal voice, as the drum-roll died away, 'I have pleasure in introducing — Anitra!'

'Who's that?' whispered Dene to Stacey.

'Anitra?'

79

'No, the fat man.'

'That's Pellissi.'

Dene looked with more interest at the proprietor of 'The Flaming Dawn'. His hair was almost black and very carefully waved. The waves were too perfect and regular to be natural. His face was olive-hued with a pouting mouth and over-red lips. Everything about him was over done. The immaculate evening dress fitted too well, the white tie was too perfectly tied. An unpleasant type, thought Dene, suave, possibly cruel, and capable of anything.

The lights went down as the drummer began another prolonged roll and a spotlight from a small balcony focussed on a curtained arch at the rear of the band platform. There was a pause and then the curtain was drawn aside and a woman stepped forward into the circle of dazzling light.

She was dressed in a gown of black velvet that clung to her as though it had been painted on her, showing every curve and line of her really lovely figure. Her dark hair, which she wore loose, was of shoulder length, dressed high in front and caught back on the left side with a single blood-red rose which matched the colour of the full mouth. Her face was perfect. Dene, who had seen many lovely women, thought she had everything plus a hundred per cent.

She stood waiting while the burst of applause that had greeted her appearance died down, and then, without any acknowledgement beyond a slightly contemptuous look in her large dark eyes, walked to the microphone. She moved with an almost feline grace and the faintest trace of a swing to her velvet-sheathed hips.

And then she began to sing a blues number. Her voice was deep and slightly husky and she sang without effort. She sang three numbers and then, in the midst of the applause, she gave a slight bow, walked back to the curtained archway, turned and bowed again, still with that faintly contemptuous expression in her eyes, and backed through the archway. The curtain dropped into place in front of her and she was gone.

'That woman's an artist,' remarked Colgate-Jones, as the lights went up and the band began to play a quick-step.

'With a personality like that she could be anything,' said Dene. 'How long has she been here?'

'Ever since the place reopened,' answered Stacey. 'She is the chief attraction.'

'I wonder why she wastes her time at a place like this,' said Carol.

Stacey shrugged his shoulders.

'There are rumours that she and Pellissi — ' he stopped, but the expression of his face was eloquent.

'Surely not,' protested Carol. 'That awful little fat man?'

'Women are queer creatures,' said Colgate-Jones tritely. 'Haven't you ever noticed that it's usually the really lovely ones who have the most insignificant husbands?'

'Darling,' broke in Carol as though she were addressing a small child. 'This is quite another matter. We weren't discussing *husbands* — or were we?'

She looked at Stacey, and he shook his head with a smile.

'No, I don't think *that's* the relationship between Anitra and Pellissi,' he answered. 'In fact I don't know that there's *any* relationship. It's nothing more than a rumour.'

'Rumour is a lying jade,' said Colgate-Jones. 'It's always apt to cling to an attractive woman, like ivy.'

'The benefit of the doubt,' said Carol. 'Kupie, you're a darling!'

'Mr. Dene,' Janice Gould's voice broke into the conversation quietly and under perfect control. 'What *did* happen to Jim Clavering? Please tell me everything.'

Michael Dene hesitated.

'You needn't worry,' said the girl, smiling faintly. 'I can stand it — whatever it is.'

He told her. He told her everything except the reason why Clavering had died, and she listened quietly, her grave eyes fixed intently on his.

'I'm not really surprised,' she said when he had finished, 'although it was a shock. You see, I was more or less prepared for something . . . '

'Why?' asked Dene.

She lit a cigarette carefully before she replied, her fingers fumbling tremulously with her lighter.

'It was a letter,' she answered at last. 'I don't know what was in it — it was sealed. Jim gave it to me the last time we met — here. 'If anything should happen to me,' he said, 'get that to Frank Stacey — you know, the fellow I introduced you to the other night.' That was why I guessed — when you said . . . '

'I see.' Dene's eyes were bright. 'Where is this letter, Miss Gould?'

'In my coat,' she replied. 'Jim made me slip it in between the lining and the fur — he made a little tear and pushed it in when he saw me home. 'There are quite a lot of people who would like to get hold of that,' he said. 'Leave it there unless you have to do what I asked you.' I begged him to tell me what it was all about, but he wouldn't. 'The less you know the better,' he said. 'This is just a precaution, that's all. You have to take precautions when you are dealing with dangerous people.' '

Carol saw the tears gathering in her

eyes, but she forced them back.

'I must have that letter,' said Dene. 'When can you get it for me?'

'Now,' she answered. 'My coat is in the cloakroom. I'll go and get it now.'

She rose to her feet.

'Be careful!' whispered Michael Dene warningly. 'Don't let anyone see what you have gone for.'

She nodded, picked up her bag, and began to thread her way across the dancefloor. For a moment she stopped at the table where the grey-haired man and his companion were sitting, said something to them, and made her way to the exit.

'That's a darned plucky girl!' said Dene. 'She's got real grit.'

'She has,' said Carol. 'I think you might have broken the news a little more gently, all the same.'

'If I had,' he answered, 'she'd have broken down. I chose the way I did on purpose.'

'You were right,' agreed Colgate-Jones, nodding, 'though I'll admit it did seem rather brutal. So Clavering left a letter, eh? Well, that ought to save us a lot of trouble.'

'I hope so,' said Dene. 'Hello, our friend in the corner has vanished.'

The vicar turned casually. The man at the table near the wall was no longer there. At some period during their conversation, he must have slipped quietly away, though no one had seen his going.

'I suppose he couldn't have heard anything?' muttered Colgate-Jones, his fat, florid face a little anxious.

Dene shook his head.

'Too far away,' he said. 'We were talking practically in whispers.'

'I don't quite like it, though, do you?' said Carol seriously. 'I think I'll go and powder my nose.'

She got up quickly, and before they could stop her, was making her way rapidly to the exit.

Stacey half rose.

'Sit down!' said Michael Dene sharply. 'You can't follow her to the ladies' cloakroom!'

Rather sheepishly the other resumed his seat.

'Do you think that Miss Wray was right?' he said uneasily, 'that there's any danger . . . '

'To the other girl?' asked Dene, and shook his head. 'I don't see why there should be. They don't know anything about the letter. There's nothing very suspicious in going to the cloakroom.'

'She was a friend of Clavering's — they must know that,' muttered Colgate-Jones, 'and she's been seen talking to us . . . '

The band started a noisy swing number, and Dene watched the dancers taking the floor. There were over a dozen men in uniform amongst them. It seemed incredible to suppose that anything could happen to the girl here, and yet the vicar's words had made him doubtful. Janice Gould was in possession of dangerous information.

'Here comes Carol,' Colgate-Jones's voice broke in on his thoughts.

'Alone,' muttered Stacey.

The girl joined them with a smile and sat down, but her voice was grave as she whispered under her breath.

'She's not in the cloakroom. I can't see her anywhere!'

Dene drew in his breath sharply.

'You're sure?' he said, and Carol nodded.

'Quite! She's nowhere about. She just walked through that exit and — vanished!'

He pursed his lips, and the V between his eyes deepened.

'There are those men again!' said Colgate-Jones suddenly, and following the direction of his eyes, Dene saw the two men appear from the narrow door beside the band platform and start to walk slowly toward them. He watched them absently, his thoughts concentrated on the disappearance of Janice Gould.

'I wish one of us had gone with her,' he muttered. 'I should have done so. I could have waited outside while she fetched her coat. We . . .'

He never completed the sentence, for at that moment every light in the place went out!

The band stopped playing with a crashing discord, a woman screamed, and a babel of excited voices rose out of the pitch darkness. Michael Dene, with a sudden premonition of danger, half started to his feet. As he did so, he heard a gasp near, and a stifled cry from Carol. Hands seized his arms, and as he struggled violently, the voice of Pellissi bellowed from the blackness: 'Don't be alarmed, ladies and gentlemen, the main fuse has gone, that is all. If you will all keep still for a little while, the lights will come on again . . . '

And then something thick and suffocating was thrown over his head and the voice faded to a scarcely audible whisper. He was swung off his feet and carried swiftly through the darkness. The muffled thud of a closing door reached his ears. He was dropped roughly on to something that felt like a divan or a bed, and the pungent sickly smell of chloroform made his nostrils tingle. The cloth round his head grew damp, and he tried to hold his breath against the drug which was being poured on it. For a little while he succeeded, and then he was forced to breathe. The chloroform flooded his lungs, and his head began to spin dizzily. Desperately he tried to ward off the growing lethargy that was stealing over him, but it overcame all his efforts. He seemed to float away on a sea of air, and knew nothing more . . .

8

His first sensation, when the stupefying effects of the drug wore off, was of movement.

Gradually, as he gained more and more control of his senses, he traced this to the fact that he was in a car. The rhythmic beat of the engine and the swish of the tyres were plainly audible.

The cloth had been removed from about his head, but he could see nothing, for he was surrounded by total darkness. Neither could he move. His arms and legs had been securely bound.

He became aware, after a little while, that he was not alone in the car. A body was pressed against him, and he could hear the sound of heavy breathing.

So the others were there, too, he thought. Under cover of the darkness at 'The Flaming Dawn' they had all been whisked away. A neat trick. When the lights came on again, who would notice the absence of four people among the crowd? It had one disadvantage, however. It definitely associated the place with the people they were up against.

Dene smiled to himself in the darkness — a little grim, mirthless smile. Perhaps that didn't matter — perhaps these people were very sure that the knowledge would never be of any value.

As a natural corollary to this thought, he began to wonder where they were being taken. The car was moving at a fair speed, but it was impossible to even guess its whereabouts. The windows had been covered with some kind of dark paint, and even if they had not, it would have been difficult to see anything in the blackout.

His head ached abominably, and leaning back in the corner, he closed his eyes. They were just as useful closed as open since there was nothing to see but blackness, and it eased the pain in his head.

He fell into a partial doze, and presently, when he awoke, he felt better.

The pain in his head had diminished, and the feeling of nausea, which had troubled him, had passed away. Feeling rather cramped, he moved gingerly, and the body leaning against him shifted too.

'Who's that?' whispered the voice of Colgate-Jones huskily.

'It's me,' grunted Dene. 'I suppose they drugged you, too.'

'They did!' replied the vicar, feelingly. 'I have never experienced the effect of what is known as 'a hangover', but I'm sure it can't be any worse than this!'

'Feeling rotten, Kupie?' asked Carol. 'So'm I! What I wouldn't give for a really hot cup of tea is nobody's business!'

'We shall all get something really hot at the end of this journey, but I don't expect it'll be anything so pleasant as tea!' said Dene.

Frank Stacey's voice broke in from somewhere below them.

'Where do you think they are taking us?' he asked.

'Where are you — on the floor?' said Dene.

'Yes,' replied Stacey. 'And damned

uncomfortable. I'm wedged like a sardine.'

He suddenly remembered the presence of Colgate-Jones and began to apologize.

'Don't mind me,' interrupted the vicar. 'I feel like using a few very choice expletives myself!'

The car continued steadily on its way, running with a smoothness that suggested well-made roads. They none of them had any idea of the time, and it was impossible to hazard a guess. Stacey repeated his question concerning their possible destination, and Dene shook his head without realizing that the action was useless.

'I've no idea,' he said. 'We can only wait and see.'

By tacit consent they relapsed into silence, while the car sped swiftly onwards. Presently, after what seemed to have been an interminable time, it began to slow down. The smoothness changed to a jolting and swaying that went on for some time, and then the car stopped.

'Well, wherever it is, we're here!' grunted Dene, and then swiftly in a whisper: 'If any of you see the slightest chance of escape, take it. Never mind about the rest!'

The door of the car was jerked open, and they saw that it was still dark outside — nearly as dark as it was in the interior of the saloon. Several men came forward, and they were lifted out and carried up a short flight of steps and through a wide door into a dimly lighted hall. Dene caught a glimpse of rugs and old furniture as he was borne swiftly up a huge staircase, along a corridor, and deposited on the floor of a big, empty room, lit by a single bulb that hung from the centre of the high ceiling.

The other three were brought in, and the men who had performed their task in complete silence withdrew and locked the door.

'Not very comfortable quarters, are they?' remarked Colgate-Jones, looking about. 'I wonder where we are?'

'Somewhere in the country, I think,' murmured Carol. 'I saw a lot of trees . . . '

'It doesn't matter very much where we are,' broke in Dene; 'the most important thing is, how can we get away? Try your bonds. Perhaps you can loosen 'em.'

They tried, but after a few minutes each had to confess that they could make no impression. The cords that bound them had been tied by experts.

'Nothing doing?' asked Dene breathlessly. 'I'm afraid it's the same here. Well, we seem to have got into a nasty jam . . .'

He stopped suddenly as there came the sound of footsteps outside the door. The key rattled in the lock, the door opened, and a man came quietly into the room.

He was of medium height, and the thick overcoat he wore enhanced his bulk. Beneath his soft-brimmed hat a handkerchief entirely covered his face.

'Good evening,' he said in a low voice that was completely toneless.

'Who are you?' demanded Michael Dene, and the newcomer uttered a little throaty chuckle that for some reason made the Secret Service man's flesh crawl.

'A good many people would like to know that, Mr. Dene,' he answered gently. 'A great many people. But none of them ever will. I am nobody — a cipher and a number. I am known as X.1.'

9

'So you're X.1, are you?' remarked Michael Dene.

The other nodded slowly.

'I am,' he replied.

'I've been wanting to meet you for a long time,' continued Dene, 'a very long time.'

'Well, your wish has at last been granted, Mr. Dene,' said X.1, 'though perhaps not quite in the way you would have wished, eh?'

'Any way is better than not at all,' retorted Dene.

'You think so?' X.1 shrugged his shoulders. 'Then you should be very thankful. I'm afraid, however, that you won't — I'm very much afraid that you won't.' He gave another of the soft, throaty chuckles that in some way seemed to epitomize the unpleasantness of his personality.

97

'What do you intend to do with us?' demanded Dene, bluntly.

'Surely there is no need for a man of your intelligence to ask that?' replied the toneless voice. 'Consider the situation, Mr. Dene. Consider what you would do in similar circumstances and answer the question yourself.'

There was no need for very much consideration. There was only one answer. Dene had known the answer before he put the question. His object was merely to gain time — for what he could not have said. Only that so long as their fate was delayed there was hope.

'Except for the fact that one of my agents unfortunately bungled,' went on X.1 after a pause, 'you would not be in your present unpleasant predicament. Had he carried out his instructions properly and seen to it that the man, Clavering, was dead instead of only wounded, you would not have become a source of danger to the successful carrying out of my plan.'

Dene looked at him steadily.

'What *is* the programme?' he asked.

'So far as you and your friends are concerned?' inquired X.1 in that soft, toneless voice that was more menacing than any voice Dene had ever heard. 'I'm afraid that you will have to die. I haven't yet worked out the details of how. You must understand that this has rather been sprung on me. It is something of a problem, because your deaths must have the appearance of being natural. The murder of so prominent a member of British Intelligence would cause too great a stir, and might result in an inquiry which would be very disadvantageous to my own organization. But don't worry. I shall no doubt hit on a scheme eventually. There is no immediate hurry.'

Dene drew an inward breath of relief though his expression did not change an iota. If they were not to be killed at once there was a chance. Not very much of one, perhaps, but still a chance.

'It is seldom,' continued X.1, 'that I make a personal appearance — even such a very — er — incognito appearance as this. You know, I suppose, that even my own agents don't know me?'

'Rumour says that only one man *does* know you,' replied Dene. 'Hitler.'

X.1 inclined his head.

'Rumour is for once correct,' he said. 'This is such a very important matter that I have altered my usual policy of only directing operations. How much do you know?'

Dene shook his head.

'Not much,' he answered.

'I thought you couldn't know much,' said X.1. 'According to my information, Clavering could not have lived long enough to have imparted much. Tell me *what* you know?'

Michael Dene considered quickly. There was nothing to be gained by withholding what he knew. Unless they could discover some means of escape they would die, anyway. On the other hand, he had been studying this man's mentality, and he had decided that, like all Germans, he was as vain as the proverbial peacock. It was possible that with skilful handling he would reveal the whole scheme, just for the sheer love of displaying his own cleverness. It was worth trying, anyway. In the remote chance that they succeeded in getting away, the knowledge would be of incalculable value. Rather to the surprise of Colgate-Jones and the others, he rapidly related what they knew, omitting, however, any reference to Janice Gould and the letter.

'H'm,' commented X.1 when he had finished. 'You know rather more than I thought, and yet really very little . . . '

'I'm still under the impression that Clavering was exaggerating,' interrupted Dene, untruthfully. 'It is almost impossible that anything you could do would have the disastrous effect he hinted . . . '

'You think so?' said X.1 quickly. 'You are mistaken, Mr. Dene. If anything, Clavering *underestimated* the result. The signal which I shall give on the twenty-first of this month will set in motion certain factors which will prove decisive. Do you think that Germany would be so *certain* of an ultimate victory in this conflict if she hadn't a good reason? No, Mr. Dene. In spite of the Russian successes, in spite of the British and American success in Tunisia, Germany is undismayed. She is not afraid of an invasion of Europe, because she is prepared for it. She has planned for years down to the smallest detail for such an eventuality as is now so fast approaching, and I assure you that the plan is perfect . . . '

'But not assured of success,' said Dene with just the right amount of scepticism in his voice. 'Plans have a habit of going wrong . . . '

'This will be successful,' retorted X.1 confidently. 'It cannot fail.'

'What is supposed to happen on the twenty-first?' asked Dene.

The cold eyes above the handkerchief narrowed.

'The destruction of the British Empire,' said X.1, and for the first time there was a tinge of emotion in his colourless voice, 'and the triumph of Germany.'

'I rather gathered that that was the intention,' said Dene impatiently, 'but how do you intend to bring it about?'

'That, Mr. Dene, is, and I'm afraid must remain, my secret,' answered X.1 smoothly. 'One thing I can tell you, however. The old-fashioned methods of war have never appealed to Germany when they can be substituted by something better. To attack a country at her frontiers is obsolete. The blow, to be successful, must be struck from *inside*. It must come when it is least expected and it must be of a shattering nature. That is the modern way of making war. That is the way we overcame France.'

'Why didn't you try the same tactics with Russia?' murmured Dene.

'Because such a thing would have been impossible with modern Russia,' replied X.1. 'There is no such thing as a Fifth Column in Russia.'

'Or in Britain,' put in Dene.

'That, to use an American expression, is what you think,' retorted X.1.

'Are you suggesting that there is?' demanded Dene, and the other nodded.

'Yes, Mr. Dene. I am more than suggesting it. I am *telling* you that there is a very powerful Fifth Column in Britain,' said X.1, 'and your method of Government has fostered it. We have only used what was already there. You have allowed your people too much freedom of thought, of action, and of speech. Look at your strikes, for example. Do you think they would be tolerated in Germany in wartime? No, the strikers would be shot for treason . . . '

'We don't shoot people here — except under great provocation,' said Dene, and there was a momentary twinkle in his eyes. 'Go on, you are interesting me.'

'If you *had* shot a few more people,' answered X.1, 'the plan, which the Führer and I worked out between us, would be impossible.'

'Even without knowing what it is, I think it's impossible,' said Dene.

'It is not only possible, but practical,' replied X.1. 'If you were alive — which I regret to say you will not be — you would see it put into practice. The scheme is Germany's, but it will be carried out by your own countrymen. That is genius — to use material at hand and mould it to suit your own purpose.'

'If you would be a little more explicit,' suggested Dene, 'I might be in a better position to argue with you.'

'Is there any particular reason why we

should argue, Mr. Dene?' said X.1. 'The whole thing is prepared — everything is ready. My agents have worked indefatigably. It has taken a long time, but it is finished now. The powder barrel has been rolled into position, the fuse is laid, it only needs the signal from me to set it alight.'

'And then what?' inquired Dene.

'Destruction!' answered X.1. 'Complete and utter chaos.'

Dene shook his head and smiled — a faintly contemptuous smile.

'And that is what *you* think!' he retorted. 'Whatever your precious plan may be, it wouldn't have *that* effect.'

'Why?' asked X.1 quickly.

'Because you don't know the British people,' said Dene.

'On the contrary, Mr. Dene, I know them very well,' was the reply. 'I have lived nearly all my life in England. Does that surprise you?'

'I have learned never to be surprised at anything,' said Dene.

'A valuable asset,' agreed X.1. 'It is a pity that you will not be in a position to receive the first surprise in your life. I assure you that I have not exaggerated the result. It is as much a certainty as that the sun will rise tomorrow.'

'We all have our delusions,' murmured Dene, deliberately infusing a note of pitying condescension into his voice. But the other did not rise to the bait. For a moment he looked at Dene steadily, and then shook his head.

'Very clever, Mr. Dene,' he said, 'but it won't do — it really won't do. I am quite aware what you are trying. You think that if you appear sufficiently sceptical, I shall, to prove that you are wrong, tell you a great deal more than I intend. You are quite mistaken. I do not intend to tell you anything more.'

Dene compressed his lips. The ease with which X.1 had read his mind was not only disconcerting, but made him feel a little foolish.

'Since you have informed us that you intend to kill us,' he said, 'it wouldn't appear to matter very much what you divulge.'

'No, but I have a natural caution in these matters,' said X.1. 'There is an old saying in Yorkshire, 'Hear all and say nowt', with which I am fully in agreement.' He walked over to the door. 'I must go now,' he said, pausing on the threshold, 'but I shall be back later — when I have decided just how I am going to deal with you.'

He went out, shutting and locking the door behind him.

10

Saturday — 11.15 p.m.

There was a silence in the bare, dimly lit room when he had gone — a silence that was broken at length by Stacey.

'Well, so much for that,' he said. 'So that is the great X.1, is it?'

'Yes, we're privileged,' answered Dene. 'Nobody except Hitler knows him.'

'Well, we don't know much,' grunted Colgate-Jones. 'Would you recognize him anywhere?'

'No,' said Dene, shaking his head. 'His build is much the same as thousands of other men, and his voice was so completely colourless that it has no individuality. He described himself perfectly when he said he was a cipher.'

'You didn't get much change out of him,' remarked Colgate-Jones. 'I saw what you were trying to do and I thought at one time that it was going to work.'

'I was hoping it would,' said Dene. 'As it is, we are no nearer knowing anything definite than we were before.'

'And we've got very little time before the twenty-first,' began the vicar.

'Unless we can get out of here,' interrupted Dene, 'the twenty-first won't matter very much to us. We shall have gone the way of all flesh long before that.'

'We've got to get out of here,' said Stacey determinedly.

'Can you suggest how?' asked Dene.

'No, but surely there must be some way,' said Stacey. 'If we . . . '

'Even if we were free, what could we do to stop this thing, whatever it is, that is scheduled to happen?' demanded Colgate-Jones. 'We don't know the signal, in fact we don't know anything . . . '

'Kupie, don't get pessimistic,' broke in Carol. 'There's a lot we could try and do, anyway, and it would be something just to go on living. The signal's got something to do with toothpaste . . . '

'I know that,' said Colgate-Jones a little irritably. 'But does it help? It doesn't convey anything to me . . . '

'If only we could have got that letter which Clavering gave to Janice Gould,' muttered Stacey.

'I'm afraid we shall never see that,' said Michael Dene, 'or the girl either. They got her without a doubt, and the letter too . . .'

'If they got her, Mr. Dene,' inquired Carol, 'what have they done with her?'

'Most likely anticipated what they are going to do with us,' replied Dene.

'But why didn't they serve us all the same?' persisted the girl. 'If they could have killed Janice then and there, why didn't they kill us, too? Why kill her and go to all the trouble of bringing us here?'

'Perhaps they didn't kill her,' put in Colgate-Jones. 'Maybe . . .'

'Then why didn't they bring her along here?' demanded Carol.

'I see what you are getting at, Miss Wray,' said Dene thoughtfully. 'If they didn't kill her and they didn't bring her here, where is she?'

She nodded.

'What's the good of conjecturing?' said the vicar mildly. 'Aren't we rather wasting time? The most important thing, surely, is to try and find some way of getting out of this very nasty position . . . '

He broke off as the key rattled in the lock and the door opened to admit a large, brawny man whose battered face and thick bull-neck suggested that he might once have been a prize-fighter.

'I've come ter keep yer company,' he said with a grin that revealed a mouth full of broken yellow teeth. He shut the door behind him and walked over to a chair. 'The boss thought yer might get up ter some tricks. If anything like that was on yer mind yer can ferget it.'

He seated himself in the chair and pulling a big automatic from his pocket balanced it on his broad knee. Dene eyed him with unconcealed distaste. It had occurred to him that they might be able to assist each other in getting free, but any hope of this was put an end to by the presence of this fresh arrival. The man seemed to read his thoughts, for his ugly grin broadened.

'Thinkin' of doin' a few Houdini tricks, was yer?' he said unpleasantly. 'We was afraid yer might, an' we didn't want no trouble, see? We 'ad enough o' that gettin' yer 'ere.'

'Where are we?' asked Dene.

'Somewhere in England,' retorted the man surlily. 'I ain't givin' away no official secrets, see. No careless talk from me.'

'You look like an Englishman,' said Dene, watching him curiously.

'Never yer mind wot I am,' snarled the big man, the grin vanishing from his battered face. 'England ain't never done nothin' fer me, see, an' money's money wherever it come from. You shut yer trap, see?'

'I hear,' replied Dene quietly, and relapsed into silence. There was nothing to be gained by talking to this brute. It would be better to try and think of some way of getting free. He closed his eyes and racked his brains for some way of escape, but he could think of nothing that was even remotely practical. He was still trying to force his brain to supply a reasonable idea when a sound from outside reached his ears — a distant and very familiar sound — the undulating wail of a siren.

Colgate-Jones evidently heard it too, for he looked up.

'That's an 'alert', isn't it?' he asked.

Dene nodded, but before he could reply there came another and much nearer wailing note. It rose and fell like the legendary cry of the banshee and then faded away to silence. The uncouth gaoler got up and went over to the window. Pulling aside the blackout he peered into the darkness. After a moment he came back to his chair and sat down again.

'The searchlights are out,' he remarked. 'Dozens of 'em. I don't s'pose there'll be anythin' much. They don't come over 'ere a lot.'

From far away came the thud of a gun. It was followed by another and another, and then a continuous barrage of gunfire that grew steadily louder.

'They're getting a pretty hot reception, anyway,' grunted Colgate-Jones, and the end of his sentence was drowned by a tremendous salvo of gunfire which shook the house and made the window rattle.

'That gun-site must be fairly close,'

said Dene, and it was the big man who answered.

'T'other side o' Yoeman's Spinney — 'bout a quarter mile away,' he said uneasily. 'It ain't often they goes off . . . '

The guns thundered again, and in the momentary lull that followed there came the faint drone of a plane. It was an intermittent drone, far away but unmistakable.

'That's a Jerry,' said Carol, and the guns, far and near, began firing in one almost continuous barrage.

'There must be quite a number of 'em,' remarked Stacey, his head slightly on one side as he strained his ears to listen. 'Every gun for miles appears to be in action.'

The sinister, intermittent drone was getting louder, and Dene concluded that the plane must be almost overhead, though experience told him that it was difficult to judge from the sound. And then he heard the first bomb fall. It came whistling down, and the explosion, although it must have been a considerable distance away, made the house tremble.

As though it were a signal it was followed almost instantly by a rain of bombs. They fell in a continuous stream with scarcely a pause, the screaming rattle of one being drowned by the explosion of another. And each burst was nearer than the last.

The ugly, battered face of the big man in the chair was white and there was naked fear in his eyes. As the house shook under the continuous detonations he got up and stood irresolutely, glancing uneasily from the window to the door.

'They're gettin' pretty close, ain't they?' he muttered. 'I wish . . . '

What he wished they never knew. A thin whistle, growing rapidly louder, made him cut off the end of his sentence abruptly. Dene saw Carol look up at the ceiling apprehensively as the rushing seemed to fill the whole room. The big man, with a growled oath, turned to run to the door, and then as his hand touched the handle there was a roar of sound that split the night savagely. The window bulged inwards and a great sheet of flame filled the space where it had been. A wind, like all the tornadoes in the world concentrated in one stupendous blast, swept the room, and Dene felt himself lifted like a leaf and hurled through space. At the same moment there was a tremendous rumbling crash, and that was the last thing he remembered. A sharp pain, so agonizing that it seemed to suck away his breath, enveloped his head and shoulders, and then a great darkness and . . . silence!

11

Saturday — 9.35 p.m.

Janice Gould walked quickly across the dancefloor at 'The Flaming Dawn' with a smile on her lips and despair in her heart. Outwardly there was nothing about her to show that she had just received news that had wiped all the joy and meaning of life from her soul. Only she could feel the sinking weight in the pit of her stomach and the dull ache that seemed to spread over her whole body. It was as though she were slowly bleeding to death internally — the gentle oozing away of all desire to live. It was strange this queer dead feeling that had come over her ever since she had heard Michael Dene's quiet and emotionless voice telling her that Jim Clavering would never come to 'The Flaming Dawn' again — that Jim Clavering was dead. In some ways it was a merciful feeling — like the local anæsthetic administered by a dentist before a tooth was extracted. The pain would come later when full realization came to her. She knew that. At the moment she could not entirely grasp the fact that Jim had gone out of her life for good — that she would never see the quizzical, careless smile with which he had been wont to greet her, and the twinkle in the humorous eyes; never hear the quiet voice with the hint of raillery that ran through it like a thread on all but the most serious occasions. When he had told her about the letter had been one of them. She stopped mechanically at the table where her friends were sitting and murmured something, she wasn't aware quite what, but they seemed to accept whatever it was quite naturally, for they only smiled and nodded, and she passed on toward the exit. The crowded room might have been empty for all she knew. The people sitting at the numerous tables were just a vague blur without outline or meaning.

She reached the exit leading to the cloakroom where she had left her coat, and passed through the curtain opening.

The woman called Anitra was standing just beyond talking in low tones to the fat proprietor, Pellissi. She stopped abruptly as Janice appeared, and they both stared at her as she passed. There was a bend in the passage before the entrance to the cloakroom, and as she came to this she looked back quickly. Pellissi and Anitra had disappeared. And then she heard voices from the other side of the bend. Two men were talking in whispers, but the sound carried in that confined space and she heard quite clearly what they were saying.

'You pull the main fuse . . . under the stairs. In the dark we can get them to that room behind the band platform. Jackson will see that no one comes in . . . ' Another voice interrupted. 'All four of them?' 'Yes, you fool, of course,' whispered the first man impatiently. 'They all know too much — if we leave one we might as well leave the lot. Now, get a move on. You know where that fuse is . . . '

Janice heard the sound of movement, and for a moment thought that they were coming toward her. But she was mistaken and realized with relief that they had gone the other way.

She waited until all sounds had faded away, and then tried to decide what she ought to do. There was very little doubt as to whom they had been talking about. Michael Dene and the other three were in danger. She turned to carry out this plan and came face to face with Anitra. The woman must have come back as noiselessly as a cat for she had heard nothing. She caught her breath. There was a hard expression on Anitra's lovely face, and her eyes revealed open suspicion. As Janice tried to pass her, she caught her arm and her grip was surprisingly strong.

'What are you doing snooping about here?' she demanded, and her deep voice was harsh and without a vestige of the musical quality which, as a rule, made it so fascinating.

'I'm not snooping . . . ' began Janice.

'You are,' broke in Anitra, without removing her hold on the girl's arm. 'I've been watching you. You were standing at the bend in the passage listening to something. What were you listening to?'

'I wasn't listening to anything,' retorted Janice. 'How dare you suggest . . . '

'Stop lying,' snapped Anitra. 'You *were* listening. I was watching you . . . '

'What right have you to spy on my movements?' said Janice. 'Surely I can go to the cloakroom for my coat without asking your permission?'

'If you went to the cloakroom for your coat,' answered Anitra, 'why didn't you get it?'

'I changed my mind,' said Janice. 'Isn't one allowed to do that at 'The Flaming Dawn'?'

Anitra made no reply. With narrowed eyes she stared at the other in silence.

'Would you mind letting me go?' asked Janice quietly after a pause. 'I want to go back to my friends.'

'Oh, you do, do you?' Anitra nodded slowly, and an unpleasant smile curved her lovely mouth. 'Yes, I expect you do. But I don't think you will — not until we know a little more about you, at any rate.'

'What do you mean . . . ?' began Janice.

'I think you know very well what I

mean,' replied Anitra. 'That wide-eyed innocent stuff doesn't go down with me, so you can cut it out. You're coming for a little ride, my dear.'

'A ride?' Janice tried to drag her arm free from the woman's strong fingers, but her grip only tightened. 'Will you let me go?'

'When I know more about you,' answered Anitra, and pulled her along the passage toward the bend. 'At present you are coming with me . . .'

'Where?' asked Janice.

'You'll see,' snapped the other.

'I won't go with you.' Janice made another effort to free herself. 'Why should I?'

'Don't argue,' said Anitra curtly. 'This way.'

She almost dragged Janice round the bend and to a door that faced the entrance to the ladies' room. With her free hand she jerked it open and thrust the girl inside. There was a strong smell of cigar smoke, and she caught a momentary glimpse of a comfortably furnished office. Then as she recovered her balance from the push which Anitra had given her, the lights went out and she was groping about in total darkness. She heard Anitra somewhere near her utter an exclamation, and then her arm was gripped again.

'Keep still, I'll get a light.' Anitra whispered the words almost in her ear. The woman left her alone and the next second a faint glow shone through the darkness. It came from a little gold lighter which the other woman was holding.

'Come over here,' ordered Anitra, and Janice saw that she was standing in front of another door that almost faced the one by which they had come in.

'I won't,' cried the girl angrily. 'How dare you order me about . . .'

'Shut up, and do as you're told,' broke in Anitra. 'You and I are going to have a talk, and you'd better come willingly, otherwise there is going to be trouble. And don't try and scream, or anything like that, or you'll get hurt.'

She snapped out the lighter and a second later Janice felt her wrist gripped again. The strength of the woman was amazing. She was dragged over against her will, and a current of cold air blew in her face. She found herself suddenly outside 'The Flaming Dawn' in the dark, and heard the slam of a door.

'There are three steps down,' whispered Anitra.

It was so dark that Janice could see nothing, but somehow she managed to stumble down the steps with the assistance of her companion. She was hurried across a strip of rough ground to where a car was drawn up without lights. Her eyes were getting more accustomed to the darkness now, and she saw that it was a big car. Anitra pulled open the door to the back seat.

'Get in,' she ordered.

Janice hesitated. In the front seat she could see the blurred figure of a man crouched over the wheel. Once she was in the car there would be no hope of getting away. It was now or never.

As though she had read her thoughts, Anitra leaned forward.

'Get in,' she said again, and her voice was urgent. 'You'd better do as you're told. If you try to make a fuss and anyone comes, I shall only say that you got tight and were trying to make a scene, and that I am taking you home. I'm pretty well known here, and my story would be believed.'

'Where are you taking me?' asked Janice.

'You'll see,' was the evasive reply. 'Now, don't waste any more time. Get in.'

Janice shrugged her shoulders. There was nothing to be done, she thought, so she might as well do as Anitra demanded. It would be too late to warn her companions. Their danger had started when the lights went out, and nothing she could do now would help them. She began to feel, too, a certain amount of curiosity about Anitra. The woman was desperately frightened about something. Beneath her cold exterior was a hint of panic. It was noticeable in the tone of her voice and in the expression of her eyes. She was both frightened and suspicious. Why?

Janice discovered to her surprise that she was very curious to find out. Was Anitra connected with the men who had been responsible for the death of Jim Clavering? The possibility, which seemed even more than a possibility when she came to think of it, decided her. Without further argument she stepped into the dark interior of the car, and was followed instantly by Anitra.

Almost before the door closed and they had taken their seats, the big machine began to move forward. The driver apparently already had his instructions, which was queer. Anitra could not by any possible means have expected to find her in the passage by the ladies' cloakroom, and yet, on the face of it, it looked as though everything had been arranged beforehand. Rather mystified, Janice snuggled back in the corner of the seat and tried to puzzle it out. Now that she had been forced into this situation, she was determined to follow it through. Not, she had to admit to herself, that she had very much choice in the matter. But it gave her something to think about, and helped to alleviate that dull pain somewhere inside her that she had felt ever since Michael Dene in one short sentence had destroyed all that made life worth living. If this adventure proved to be the means of bringing the people concerned with the death of Jim Clavering to justice, then she would feel that she had at least done something towards avenging him.

The car ran smoothly out through the entrance to 'The Flaming Dawn', and turned toward Staines. Anitra lighted a cigarette, and sat back silent and completely relaxed. It was obvious that she had no intention of talking, and this suited Janice since it gave her an opportunity to think. It occurred to her as a kind of undercurrent to her real thoughts that she was cold, and as she realized that she had nothing over her rather inadequate evening frock, she remembered that her fur coat was still in the cloakroom at 'The Flaming Dawn', and that it still contained the letter which Jim had given her. She frowned. It had been a mistake to leave that behind. It had been of the very utmost importance. She ought to have made an effort to get her coat before allowing Anitra to whisk her away on this mysterious excursion. But events had happened so quickly, and she had been so full of her intention to warn Dene and his companions of the danger that threatened them, that she had momentarily forgotten the original reason for her being near the cloakroom at all. Now that she had remembered, it was too late.

The car sped on swiftly and almost noiselessly. The swish of the tyres as they kissed the road was the only sound. The high-powered engine made no noise at all, or it was so slight that it was inaudible above the other sound.

After about twenty minutes the car suddenly slowed, and turned through an open white gate. Janice guessed at a curving drive, and then they drew up in front of a low white house that showed dimly in the darkness.

As the car stopped, Anitra opened the door and got out, waiting for Janice to join her. The girl did so, and Anitra said something in a low voice to the driver. The car moved off, turned on the semi-circle of gravel before the house, and disappeared in the direction from whence they had come.

Anitra fumbled in her bag, found a key, and jerking her head to indicate that Janice should precede her, mounted the shallow steps that led up to the covered portico. She inserted the key, gave it a quick twist, and the front door swung open.

'Go in, and keep still. I'll put the light on,' said Anitra, and Janice stepped into the hall. She heard the door close, and then there was a click and a soft light came on. Looking curiously round she saw that she was standing in a wide square room that was half hall and half lounge. There was a big red brick fireplace at one end, and in front of this was a large comfortable looking settee and two deep and inviting easy-chairs. Near the fireplace was a long window, the curtains to which were drawn. The place was quietly and expensively luxuriant.

Anitra went over to the fireplace, and switched on an electric fire.

'Sit down,' she invited, waving her hand toward the settee. 'I'll get you a drink.'

'I'd rather not have a drink,' answered Janice.

'Nonsense,' retorted Anitra, busy at a cocktail cabinet, 'a drink will do you good. You look frozen. You needn't imagine that I'm going to drug you or poison you. This is pre-war Scotch.'

She poured out two drinks, brought one over to Janice, and went back to the cabinet against which she leaned sipping her own drink and staring at Janice thoughtfully.

The girl returned her stare steadily.

'Well,' she said at last, 'you've forced me to come here. Now, perhaps, you'll tell me why?'

'You do it very well, I must say that,' remarked Anitra.

'I don't know what I do very well,' retorted Janice, 'but thanks for the compliment.'

'Yes, you do it extremely well,' repeated Anitra, taking another sip from the long glass in her hand. 'Now just tell me what the game is?'

'I don't know what you're talking about,' said Janice.

'Very well, I'll put it another way.' Anitra drained her whisky and set the empty glass down carefully on the cabinet beside her. 'What do you know?'

Janice smiled.

'That's rather a sweeping question, isn't it?' she said. 'I know quite a lot really.'

'I thought you did.' Again Anitra's eyes narrowed and she nodded to herself slowly. 'Ever since you've been coming to 'The Flaming Dawn' I've thought you weren't just one of the usual habitués of such a place. I thought you were there for a purpose, and it appears you were. Who were the people with you tonight?'

'Just friends of mine,' replied Janice. All her senses were alert and she was choosing her words carefully. If she were clever Anitra would give herself away. Janice had at present no idea what she was talking about, but she guessed that if she waited and said as little as possible the woman would tell her. In this she may have been right, but the opportunity was not to present itself then, for Anitra had opened her mouth to say something further when there was the sound of a key in the lock of the front door, and as Janice turned to see who had entered, she looked into the fat, angry face of Pellissi!

12

Michael Dene seemed to swim up out of a sea of silence and blackness into an inferno of sound and flickering light. At first he was bewildered and puzzled. There was a racking pain somewhere in the region of his neck and shoulders — a pain that was part of him and yet at the same time curiously detached. He felt that he was no longer a solid entity, but just a mind floating in space without any material body. Except that pain which came intermittently. After a little while he became vaguely aware of things that were going on around him. There were lights flickering and dancing in darkness — orange and red lights that flared and died and flared again, and intermingled with the lights was a queer hissing sound that reminded him in some curious way of a railway station. Dark figures flitted to and

133

fro and in and out of a kind of fog — a shifting fog that was very dense at one minute and gone altogether the next. In one of these moments of visibility he saw the bright tongues of a huge fire, and became aware of an acrid tang in the air that made his nostrils tingle and his eyes smart. And then, very slowly and gradually, he began to remember. The bare room in the big house . . . the sound of sirens and the guns . . . the explosion of the falling bombs. There had been one tremendous explosion, and then pain and utter blankness . . .

'Hello, feelin' better?'

A voice came out of the mist of smoke. A figure wearing a tin-helmet, which gleamed in the flickering light, bent down. Dene saw that the man was dressed in the dark blue uniform of the Civil Defence.

'Yes,' he replied huskily and weakly.

'Yer blinkin' lucky ter be alive, chum,' went on the voice, 'an' no bones broke neither. All you've got's a whackin' great bruise on yer right shoulder, an' a bit of a bump on yer 'ead.'

'I suppose I am lucky,' agreed Dene. 'There were two other men and a girl with me — what happened to them?'

'They are lucky too,' answered the man. 'You was all lucky. The ambulance orter be 'ere any minute now.'

'Are you in charge here?' inquired Dene, and the other shook his head.

'No,' he answered. 'Mr. Warren's in charge.' He looked round. 'That's 'im over there.' He called to a figure that had loomed out of the smoke. 'Hi! Mr. Warren, sir. One of these blokes 'as come round.'

The figure advanced toward them. He was, as Dene could see in the uncertain light from the fire, a big, stoutish man. His face was streaming with sweat and almost black with grime.

'Feeling better?' he asked as he stooped over Dene. 'I thought you were a goner when we brought you out.'

'I'm feeling much better,' replied Dene. 'Tell me, how many were saved?'

'Two men and a girl beside yourself,' said Warren. He stooped closer. 'There's something I'd like you to explain, sir.

135

When we found you, you were tied hand and foot. So were the other two men and the girl. What was the idea?'

'Not mine,' said Dene. 'I think we'd better have a little talk, Mr. Warren. Nobody else was saved in there?' He nodded toward the burning building.

The other shook his head.

'No, sir,' he answered, and there was curiosity in the look he gave Dene. 'There were three other men beside you and your — your friends. Two of them were in the lower part of the house and the rest collapsed on them. The other had his back broken. It's a miracle you four escaped without any serious injury. You can put it down to the fact that the ceiling of the room you were in fell almost in one piece. It formed a protective guard over you, if you understand what I mean.'

'How are my friends?' asked Dene.

'The girl is still unconscious,' said Warren. 'She had rather a heavy blow on her head. But the other two are practically unhurt. They are looking after her.'

Dene raised himself cautiously on his

elbow, found that beyond a momentary dizziness he was all right, and got slowly to his feet. He swayed for a moment and Warren slipped a strong hand under his arm.

'Take it easy, sir,' he advised.

'I'm all right,' muttered Dene. The faintness cleared and he stood, a little groggily, but still fairly sure of himself. 'Take me over to my friends,' he said.

Warren led the way away from the burning house to a grassy mound that was evidently part of the garden. Here they found Colgate-Jones and Stacey administering to Carol, who had apparently just recovered consciousness.

The vica's face was blackened by smoke, and Stacey was not much better. Both their clothes were torn and they looked like scarecrows. Carol had come off little better. Of the dress she had been wearing very little remained. Her stockings were in shreds, and her hair was full of dust and debris. Stacey had been bathing a cut on her forehead with water, and this had streaked her make-up until she presented a curious mottled appearance.

'You all look like the morning after the night before,' remarked Michael Dene, as he surveyed the group.

'You don't look so good yourself,' grunted Colgate-Jones, looking up, 'but I'm glad to see you all the same. They told us you were all right, and so we decided to look after Carol as she seemed hurt the most.'

'I'm all right, Kupie,' said the girl. 'I've felt worse after a binge.'

'What a night!' said Stacey. 'Just one exciting thing after another.'

'A very lucky night, all the same,' said Dene.

'Lucky!' repeated Colgate-Jones. 'Well, I suppose in a way you're right. We're lucky to be alive.'

'That and the fact that all the others in that house are not,' said Dene. 'And while we're on the subject — we are not alive!'

They stared at him.

'Are you quite sure you're feeling all right?' asked Colgate-Jones anxiously.

'I'm feeling quite all right,' replied Dene. 'Don't you see what I'm driving at? This is a heaven-sent opportunity if we play the cards we have been presented with properly. X.1 and the rest of the bunch know we were in that house. They will know, if they don't know already, that the place was destroyed by a bomb in the raid. All their own men were killed, so why shouldn't we have been, too? There's nobody to say we weren't — in fact, I will have it put abroad that *everyone* in the house was killed. That frees us from any more attentions from X.1 and leaves us to work quietly in the dark to uncover this plot.'

Stacey pursed up his lips in a silent whistle.

'I see the idea,' he said. 'It's a jolly good one.'

'But I can't just disappear,' protested Colgate-Jones. 'What's going to happen to my parish? The Bishop will have a fit . . . '

'You leave the Bishop to me,' said Dene. 'This is a question of the safety of the country, and the Bishop will have to fall into line. Don't worry about that.'

Warren, who had been standing listening in growing astonishment, now intervened.

'Would you mind telling me what all this is about, sir?' he asked.

'I intend to,' answered Dene. 'Come over here.'

He led the way to an open space where there was no possibility of an eavesdropper.

'Now listen, and listen carefully,' he began in a low voice. 'The future of your country rests on you carrying out what I'm going to ask you to do.'

As quickly as possible he explained the whole situation to the wondering and amazed Warren, and when he had finished produced a certain document he carried, signed with a very illustrious name, which gave him full authority to act as he thought fit in an emergency.

'This constitutes an emergency,' he concluded. 'You can check up on my bona-fides at any police-station, but you can act first and check up after. If this is to be successful we've no time to waste.'

'All right, sir.' Warren was quick to make up his mind. 'I'll take your word for the time being. No harm can be done, anyway, in suppressing the fact that you and your friends are still alive.'

'What about your men?' asked Dene. 'Can they be relied on?'

'You could trust them with your life, sir,' was the prompt reply.

'I'm doing more than that, I'm trusting them with my death!' retorted Dene, and the Civil Defence man grinned. 'Now, where is the nearest police-station? I shall want a car to get away from this place. By the way, what *is* this place?'

'Sythe, sir,' answered Warren. 'It's a small village just outside Oxford. The nearest police-station is in Oxford.'

'How far is that?' inquired Dene.

'About seven miles,' answered Warren, and then as Dene's brows wrinkled he added quickly, 'I can get you there, sir. One of our cars'll take you.'

Dene's face cleared.

'That's fine,' he said. 'And the sooner the better. When can we start?'

'Now, if you want,' replied Warren. 'I'll go and fix it up.'

He hurried away into the murk of

smoke, and Dene rejoined the others.

'What happens after we get to Oxford?' demanded Colgate-Jones.

'We, or rather I, explain the matter to the local police, borrow a car and drive as fast as we can to Datchet,' said Dene. 'There's a man living there who will look after us for as long as we wish. He's a queer sort of bloke, but he's thoroughly trustworthy. He's done some work for me before.'

'I don't care where we go,' declared Carol fervently, 'so long as I can get a bath, something to eat, and a bed. I look dreadful, I'm starving, and I should like to sleep for a week!'

'You shall have all three things,' said Dene. 'I don't know about sleeping for a week, but you shall have a good rest, anyhow. Buncle has a very nice little house which he looks after entirely himself. He's an excellent cook — '

'Let's get there as soon as possible, sir,' interrupted Stacey. 'I could eat a house.'

'Well,' remarked Colgate-Jones with a twinkle in his eye, 'I put myself entirely in your hands, Dene. You deal with the Bishop and I'll do anything you want me to.'

'And like it,' put in Carol. 'You're a humbug, Kupie! You know you'd much rather chase spies all over England than preach a sermon.'

The vicar sighed.

'There's some truth in what you say, my dear,' he answered apologetically. 'I've got the spirit of adventure in my blood, I'm afraid.'

'Well, you're likely to have all you want and a bit more before we are through with this business,' said Dene. 'We've got to work against time, and however exciting that may sound in stories, it's not so funny in real life.'

Warren reappeared at that moment, emerging through the thinning smoke rather like a jinn from a bottle, to announce that the car was waiting. They followed him to where it stood, and Carol, Stacey, and Colgate-Jones climbed wearily into the back seat. Dene, after saying goodbye to Warren, got in beside the driver, and the machine shot away into the night.

They were a silent party during the

short journey. Dene was busy with his own none too pleasant thoughts, and the others were tired. Carol curled herself up in the corner of the seat and was asleep almost before the car had started.

It took them about half an hour to do the run from Sythe, and Dene was nodding himself when they pulled up in front of the police-station at Oxford.

He went in, made known his identity to the desk sergeant, and was conducted to the inspector in charge. Once again he produced his credentials and explained what he wanted. The sight of the warrant he carried galvanized the inspector into activity. Twenty minutes after his arrival he was sitting at the wheel of a police car, driving slowly down the High Street at Oxford *en route* for the residence of the eccentric Mr. Buncle.

The night, or what remained of it, was very dark, and he was forced to drive carefully. He took the opportunity that offered, to try and clarify his thoughts. He was no nearer to achieving his object than he had been earlier that evening, but he was in a better position for investigating what lay behind Clavering's last words and the plot hatched by X.1. He could no longer be worried by the attentions of that elusive and unknown individual. X.1, and those serving him, were, or soon would be, under the impression that he was dead, and that all knowledge of the existence of a plot had died with him. It *might* have the effect of making them careless, but it would, anyway, give him a free hand to work in the dark. He could not count on them being careless, but there was just a chance that they might be. The whole difficulty lay in the time element. Before the twenty-first of that month — just seven days from then — he had to find out what the plot was and render it harmless. And he had nothing whatever to go on, nothing except those disjointed last words of Clavering's, and they conveyed nothing to him. What was the meaning of 'toothpaste' in connection with the plot? That it concerned the signal which X.1 would give to set the whole thing in motion he knew, but how was it going to do that? How did it act? What possible use could toothpaste have in supplying the signal? He could find no sensible answer to this question. There was not enough data to go on. Without some knowledge of the plot it was impossible to conjecture how toothpaste came into it. The difficulty was going to be to find out anything in the short time at his disposal. There was just no clue on which to even begin to work. It was doubtful if a visit to 'The Flaming Dawn' would produce any real result, and even that he could not undertake personally, since to do so would be to give away the fact that he was still alive. He could only continue to think until he reached one of those flashes of inspiration which had served him in good stead in the past, and which might give him a jumping-off point. That was really all he wanted — just somewhere to begin. At the moment he felt rather like a blind man in a fog groping his way round and round in circles and coming back to the same starting point having achieved nothing.

It was nearly three o'clock when, tired and weary, he brought the car to a halt outside the white gate of a low, rambling house on the outskirts of Datchet. Getting stiffly down from behind the wheel, he opened the gate and walked up the short path of crazy paving bordered on either side by a neat hedge of privet. He paused for a moment under the overhanging green-painted porch, and then rang the bell. He heard it shrill its summons somewhere inside the house, and after waiting a moment heard the rumble of a window-sash as it was raised from somewhere above.

Stepping back, he looked up and saw that the window to the right and above the porch had been opened and a tousled head thrust out.

'Who is it? What is it?' demanded a high-pitched voice shrilly.

'It's me — Dene,' answered Dene. 'Don't make a song and dance about it, Buncle. Come down and open the door.'

'Good God!' exclaimed the shrill voice in astonishment. 'I'm coming — I'm coming!'

The window was slammed down, and presently Dene heard the shuffle of slippered feet from inside the house. Bolts shot back with a rattle and the door was opened to reveal a very small man clad in a long, white nightgown that appeared to be several sizes too large for him.

'Come in, Mr. Dene — come in,' invited Mr. Buncle in the high-pitched voice that seemed to be part and parcel of his personality. 'This is an unexpected pleasure, most unexpected.'

'You don't know how unexpected, Buncle,' agreed Dene. 'Look, I've got three friends outside in the car. Can you put us all up for a few days? I'll explain why later.'

'Certainly, certainly,' replied Mr. Buncle without a moment's hesitation, as though putting up a few friends in the middle of the night were a common occurrence. 'Bring them in, Mr. Dene, bring them in. Any friends of yours always welcome.'

Dene thanked him and, turning, went back to the car. Carol, Colgate-Jones, and Stacey were fast asleep, but they woke up with surprising alacrity when he told them that they had arrived at their destination.

'Food!' mumbled Carol, yawning and

rubbing her eyes. 'Food.'

'Hear, hear!' said Stacey, his voice husky with sleep. 'Food and bed. That's all I want in this world at the moment.'

'Then your wishes will be granted in a few minutes,' said Dene. 'I wish that was all I wanted.'

They tumbled out of the car and followed him up the little path. When they opened the door they saw that Mr. Buncle, with the true instincts of a host, had switched on a light in the hall. It was a rather attractive light, consisting of an old ship's lantern of polished copper which hung from a beam in the centre of the low roof. The hall itself was attractive, too. Carol, who had an eye for such things, thought she had seldom seen a more attractive hall, at any rate in so small a house. It was almost square in shape and very, very neat. The floor was of polished oak blocks, black with age, and gleaming like glass. Strewn over these were several rugs, their ancient colours dim, so that they blended with their background warmly. A big jug of copper stood in one corner under the stairway, filled with rust-coloured chrysanthe-mums. Under the one long window, which occupied one wall, was a settle of dark oak that looked like a genuine antique. Two chairs, covered in old chintz that would have been quite unobtainable in these days, completed the furniture. There were several very ancient plates on the walls, some old china that looked like real willow-pattern, and one or two old brasses, combining to make a very attractive picture.

Their host, who had pulled on a coat over the old-fashioned nightgown without doing anything to hide its incongruity, came forward to greet them.

He was, Carol thought, the oddest looking man she had ever seen. He was only about four feet six inches high, and his small figure looked too frail to support his large head, which seemed to weigh him down. It was a well-shaped head, with a high, intelligent brow, but it was marred by his hair, which grew in tufts regardless of anything approaching sym-metry. It sprang all over the domed scalp, like weeds that have been scattered on a patch of bare ground, and it was of a peculiar and unpleasant shade of ginger interspersed with grey. It gave Mr. Buncle a queer piebald appearance. His eyes were his best feature. They were large and liquid, and of a brown shade that was almost a deep chestnut. Carol thought that there was something very attractive about them and wondered what it was until it suddenly came to her that they were like the eyes of a faithful dog.

'I am very happy to receive you,' remarked this strange individual. 'If you will come into the sitting room and sit down, I will go and prepare a meal. I am sure that you are hungry.'

'We're ravenous, Mr. Buncle,' said the girl.

'Come this way,' invited Mr. Buncle, opening a door that led off the hall, 'and make yourselves comfortable while I see what I can find for you.'

They followed him into a large, low-ceilinged room that was as attractive as the hall, and furnished with odd pieces of period furniture that in some strange way blended. The only thing modern about the entire furniture were the two easy-chairs and the big, deep-cushioned settee that occupied a position in front of the wide, open fireplace.

Mr. Buncle motioned them to be seated and silently withdrew, closing the door behind him.

'What a queer-looking man,' said Stacey, sinking into a chair with a sigh of relief.

'He certainly is unusual to look at,' agreed Colgate-Jones, gazing round the room appreciatively, 'but he knows how to make himself comfortable.'

'He certainly does,' said Carol with a prodigious yawn. 'Oh gosh. I'm so tired.'

'Although he may not look it,' said Dene, 'Buncle is a very clever man. He may be able to help us quite a lot.'

Mr. Buncle reappeared at that moment, or rather his head did, round the door.

'It has occurred to me,' he remarked, 'that you might like to have a wash before you partake of refreshment. If so, I will show you the way to the bathroom.'

'Lead me to it,' said the girl fervently.

'We'll go in relays,' said Colgate-Jones. 'You go first, Carol.'

The girl got up and disappeared with Mr. Buncle. After a short interval she re-appeared looking more like her normal self.

'The bathroom's lovely,' she announced, 'and the water's boiling. I'd have loved a bath, but I resisted the temptation out of consideration for the rest of you.'

'Thank you,' said Dene. 'Come along, you two, we may as well all go together — it will save time.'

They found that Carol's description of the bathroom had not been exaggerated. It was large and beautifully fitted. There was a shower and everything necessary for the comfort of the toilet.

'Once again I say that your friend Buncle knows how to make himself comfortable,' remarked Colgate-Jones, as he prepared to get some of the grime off himself.

'The house is his hobby,' said Dene. 'For years now he has devoted himself to nothing else.'

By the time they had finished washing and returned to the sitting room, the meal, which the remarkable Mr. Buncle had been getting ready, was waiting. Although that individual was profuse in his apologies concerning it, it was really good, consisting of excellent omelettes followed by stewed fruit and custard.

'I expect you're full of curiosity,' said Dene, when they had finished. 'But we've all had a pretty trying time tonight, and I think it would be better if we postponed explanations until the morning. I for one can scarcely keep my eyes open.'

Mr. Buncle nodded his queer head.

'I will take you to your rooms whenever you are ready,' he said. 'We will talk tomorrow.'

'Yes,' said Dene, 'we will talk tomorrow. There's a lot to talk about, Buncle.'

Mr. Buncle's large brown eyes regarded him gravely.

'Perhaps there will be more to do than only talk?' he suggested, hopefully.

'Much more,' said Dene. 'There's quite a difficult problem to solve, and there isn't much time to do it.'

'I hope,' said Mr. Buncle, rather like a small boy asking to be allowed to go to a party, 'that you will let me help?'

'That's why we came here,' replied Michael Dene.

13

Pellissi stood still for a moment in silence surveying Janice and then he turned to Anitra.

'What do you think you're doing?' he snarled. 'Why have you brought this girl here?'

'I caught her spying . . . ' began the woman, but he interrupted her with an angry gesture.

'You fool!' he cried. 'You *bloody* fool!'

Anitra's dark eyes blazed suddenly.

'Don't you dare to talk to me like that!' she snapped furiously. 'Who the hell do you . . . '

'Think I am, eh?' finished Pellissi, flinging his hat into a corner. 'I'll tell you who I am. I'm running this business, see. I'm the boss and I'm not standing for any interference from you, see. I planned everything, and I don't intend to have my plans messed up by your damned stupidity . . . '

'*You* planned everything?' Anitra had recovered her temper. There was still a glint in her eyes, but her manner was cool and contemptuous. Janice had a sudden feeling that she had become infinitely more dangerous.

'Yes, I.' Pellissi advanced a few steps farther into the lounge. 'If it was not me, who was it? You never planned anything; you couldn't plan. All you did was to carry out my instructions. That was all right. Now you have started to think for yourself, and you have nearly ruined everything.'

Anitra took a cigarette from a box and lit it slowly. Her long fingers were trembling a little as she strove to suppress her anger.

'You talk a lot,' she said, blowing a thin stream of smoke from the corner of her mouth, which had curved into a sneer.

'*I* talk a lot?' Pellissi spread his fat hands. 'And why? Isn't there reason to talk a lot? Look what you have done . . . '

'I have done the only thing that was

possible to do,' retorted Anitra. 'If you can't see that, you must be half-witted.'

'But why didn't you come to me first?' he demanded. 'You could not do that, could you? You must act on your own and spoil everything . . . '

'Would you mind telling me what all this is about?' broke in Janice impatiently. 'I have been brought here against my will and accused of spying for no reason at all as far as I can see . . . '

'You *were* spying,' said Anitra. 'You were lurking about the corridor near the ladies' cloakroom, listening and watching. I saw you myself.'

'I was doing nothing of the sort,' protested Janice angrily. 'I've told you that before . . . '

'Please, please.' Pellissi came over to the settee. 'There has been a mistake — just a little mistake. It can be put right . . . '

'What are you talking about?' demanded Anitra. 'There has been no mistake. I know that this girl was spying, I tell you. If you do anything foolish, we shall both land in prison, and I don't intend to . . . '

Pellissi swung round on her furiously.

'Will you be quiet?' he exclaimed. 'Cannot you hold your tongue?'

'I don't intend to hold my tongue while you get us both landed in gaol!' said Anitra. 'You're not the only person concerned in this business, even if the way you talk might lead anyone to suppose you were. I'm in it, too, and I'm going to look after myself . . .'

'A good way you go about looking after yourself, eh?' said Pellissi. 'You do this stupid thing and call it looking after yourself? You are mad — stark raving mad.'

'I am beginning to think you're both mad,' said Janice. 'Now, do you mind continuing your conversation after I've gone? I'm very tired and . . .'

'You're not going until you have told the truth,' interrupted Anitra.

'You can't keep me here . . .' began Janice.

'That's what you think!' snapped the woman.

'Now listen,' broke in Pellissi. 'Miss Gould is right. You can't keep her here . . .'

'Now who's being the fool?' demanded Anitra. 'What do you think will happen if we let her go? I'll tell you. She'll talk, and we shall have all sorts of people making inquiries. If you let her go you might as well throw everything up and clear out before they come and arrest you. I should, anyway.'

For the first time Pellissi seemed impressed with her argument.

'There is some sense in what you say,' he muttered, frowning. 'Yes, she cannot be allowed to go . . . '

'You surely don't intend to keep me here against my will?' protested Janice.

'My dear young lady' — Pellissi smiled in what he obviously hoped was an ingratiating manner. 'My *dear* young lady, I regret the necessity, but I am afraid we have no alternative. It is as Anitra has said. If we let you go you would talk about this little — er — party, and there would be trouble for us. Yes, there would be a lot of trouble. We cannot afford to take the risk. I am afraid you will have to stay here for a few days — only for a few days. After that it will not matter.'

'I'm glad you're getting some sense at last,' remarked Anitra, crushing out the stub of her cigarette.

'Well, you may call it sense,' said Janice, 'but I think it's just silly. I don't know what this is all about, but it sounds like something out of a thriller.'

'Maybe that is just what it is,' said Anitra, and although she was smiling as she spoke, there was no mirth in her smile. It was just a mechanical contraction of the facial muscles and never reached her eyes, which at that moment were remarkably hard.

'You will be made comfortable, do not fear,' said Pellissi. 'There is a very comfortable room at the top of the house . . . '

'It can remain comfortable and empty, as far as I am concerned,' said Janice calmly. 'I think this nonsense has gone far enough. I am going.'

She got up and brushed down her dress.

'You are not going,' said Anitra quietly. 'You are going to do as you are told. Perhaps in the morning you will feel like telling the truth. I want to know who put you up to this.'

'Now,' said Pellissi hastily, 'let me handle this if you please. We do not intend you any harm, dear lady, but we are engaged in a very delicate — er — business transaction and the slightest — what shall I say — interference perhaps is as good a word as any — would spoil the work of months. So you understand, it is just a precaution we take, nothing more. You will be well treated — we do not wish you any harm . . .'

'Oh, cut the soft soap!' snapped Anitra impatiently. 'She's going to stop whether she likes it or not, so what's the use of wasting breath.'

'There are ways of doing these things,' murmured Pellissi. 'I prefer the nice way. If Miss Gould will honour us by being our guest for a few days it will be better than . . .'

'Oh, call a spade a spade!' said Anitra. 'Come on, I'll take you up to your room . . .'

'Supposing I refuse to go?' demanded Janice.

'You wouldn't do that, I'm sure,' answered Anitra. 'It would be an unfortunate thing from your point of view.'

'Miss Gould will be reasonable,' said Pellissi, his greasy, fat face wreathed in a smile. 'There will be no need to use any form of coercion. It would hurt me if we had to resort to anything of that kind.'

'But not nearly so much as it would hurt you!' said Anitra to the girl. 'So you'd better be sensible and come with me.'

Janice looked from one to the other. It would be useless to try and put up a fight. The odds were two to one. And then it struck her that perhaps if she pretended to agree she might learn quite a lot that would have a bearing on Jim Clavering's death. That was still at the back of her mind — had been ever since she had heard the news from Dene. And she was convinced, now, that these two were mixed up in it. She made up her mind.

'Well,' she said, shrugging her shoulders, 'since you're anxious for my company it would be impolite to refuse . . . '

'I knew you would be a sensible young

lady,' exclaimed Pellissi delightedly. 'You will suffer no inconvenience, I assure you . . .'

'Except that you won't be allowed to leave your room,' said Anitra shortly. 'Now let's cut the cackle and get to bed.'

She went over to the foot of the stairway, jerking her head towards Janice as a sign for the girl to follow her. She did so, and Anitra led the way up to the floor above. At the end of a corridor she paused and opened a door on the right. Going in, she switched on a light, revealing a small, comfortably furnished bedroom.

'There you are,' she said ungraciously. 'Make yourself as comfortable as you can, because you are going to stay for quite a long time.'

'Everything shall be done to make your visit as pleasant as possible, Miss Gould,' said Pellissi, who had come up behind them. 'Anitra, you will, perhaps, find Miss Gould something in which to sleep?'

'I'll lend her something,' said Anitra. 'You stay and watch her until I get back.'

She walked quickly away down the

corridor, and Pellissi leaned up against the open doorway.

'I am sorry for this necessity, Miss Gould,' he remarked. 'It is a most unpleasant thing for me to have to ask of you, but I cannot help myself. Much depends on this business which I am negotiating. There will be money — a very great deal of money — for myself and Anitra, so you must understand that we have to avoid the risks.'

'I don't understand anything,' retorted Janice shortly.

'It is better so,' said Pellissi, nodding his head. 'It is much better that you should not understand. Do not try, my dear young lady. Just accept the position and be content to remain our guest for a little while. We will do everything that is possible for your comfort, of this I assure you. Anitra, she is hasty in the temper and impulsive, but she is a good girl really. If you behave amiably she will be all right.'

There was a hidden note of warning conveyed in his words — a warning that was underlined and accentuated by the look he directed at her.

'How long do you intend to keep me a prisoner here?' demanded Janice.

'A prisoner? That is an ugly word.' Pellissi spread his hands and looked at her with his head on one side. 'Do not think of it in that way. How long? Well, that depends. There are many things on which it will depend. I will arrange for Anitra to have a little talk with you tomorrow and then we will see.'

Before Janice could reply Anitra came back. She carried a filmy nightdress over her arm, which she flung down on the bed.

'There you are,' she said. 'Now I'm going to bed. I'll see you in the morning.'

Pellissi bowed and politely said 'Good night', and then the door was shut and Janice heard the key turn in the lock.

Well, that was that!

She suddenly felt unutterably tired and weary. The excitement of the past few hours had momentarily taken her mind off the thought of Clavering, but now he came rushing back to fill her whole being with a sense of emptiness and loss.

She sank down on the edge of the

single bed and her eyes filled with tears. She felt appallingly lonely and dispirited. Nothing seemed to matter very much now that he was dead. She felt that everything was unreal, and that she was passing through some dreadful nightmare from which she had not the power to wake herself. The only thing that was real was the heavy weight at her heart and the dull pain that it brought. For a long time she sat motionless, the tears running softly down her cheeks and falling unchecked into her lap, and then she roused herself. She might as well go to bed, she decided. She was thoroughly tired and there was a possibility that she would sleep.

Before undressing she made an examination of the room. It was quite small and very comfortable. She had nothing to grumble at regarding its comfort. Putting out the light she went over to the window, drew aside the heavy curtains, and looked out. The night was very dark and she could see little. Cautiously she opened the window and tried to lean out, but something stopped her, and she found that iron bars set closely together ran from top to sill. There was no escape that way, she concluded, and closing the window redrew the curtains and put on the light again.

As she slowly undressed she came to the conclusion that there was no point in escaping. At the moment she had learned nothing of the things which she had set out to discover, but she was in a good position. She had penetrated to the very centre of the enemy's camp, and there was every possibility that she would learn what she was determined to find out — who had been responsible for Jim Clavering's death. The thought was soothing and it stayed with her until she fell into a troubled and restless sleep.

14

Sunday — 9.30 a.m.

Michael Dene woke from a heavy, dreamless sleep and looked at his watch. It was nine o'clock and, to judge by the pale sunlight that was pouring into his room, a fine morning. He got up and, sitting on the edge of the bed, stretched himself gingerly. He was still feeling stiff and sore from the effects of the bomb explosion, but less tired. From somewhere down below he could hear the rattle of cups, and, when he opened the door to go to the bathroom, a delicious smell of freshly made coffee came wafting up to him. Evidently the eccentric Mr. Buncle was preparing breakfast.

He shaved and took a hot bath, and by the time he was dressed felt almost his normal self. Making his way downstairs to the sitting room he discovered his host laying the table. Mr. Buncle, looking a little less like some animated cartoon from a comic strip, in a neat suit of tweeds, greeted him politely.

'I slept very well and I feel as fit as a fiddle,' said Dene in reply to his solicitous inquiries. 'I suppose the others are still asleep?'

Mr. Buncle supposed they were. At any rate, he had neither seen nor heard anything of them.

'Let them rest,' said Dene. 'It may be a long time before they get any more. This is a tricky and difficult business, Buncle.'

Mr. Buncle's large brown eyes showed his interest. He suggested, diffidently, that they should have their breakfast, which was all ready, and that during it Dene might like to inform him as to the nature of the 'tricky and difficult business'.

Dene agreed that this was an excellent idea, and over bacon, tomatoes, toast, and coffee gave a detailed account of the events which had eventually brought him to Mr. Buncle's hospitable residence.

Mr. Buncle listened without interruption until he had finished. Then he produced from his pocket a cigarette-case, held it out to Dene, took a cigarette himself, and when he had carefully lighted both with a lighter, blew out a thin stream of smoke and nodded his large head gravely.

'It is, as you say, Mr. Dene,' he remarked, 'a very tricky and difficult business. You have nothing at all to go on except these disjointed last words of Clavering's, the meaning of which you do not know.' He paused and examined the red tip of his cigarette with great concentration. 'This plot, planned by the Reich and destined to be put into action in six days' time, might be anything,' he continued. 'It is obviously of great magnitude and, although X.1 no doubt exaggerates the results, it could conceivably have disastrous effects at the present moment. Germany has, no doubt, been waiting for the right moment to put it into action, and that right moment is obviously now. The victory in Africa, the change of front in Italy, and the tremendous success of Russia, coupled with the continuous and increasing bombing raids on Germany itself, must have proved damaging to the German morale — the morale of the people. Something has got to be done to bolster that up. With this card up their sleeve it is not surprising that the Germans are more confident of ultimate victory than events seem to warrant. You have no idea what form this attack from within will take?'

Dene shook his head.

'Not the remotest,' he declared. 'An epidemic of some fatal disease — sabotage on a wholesale scale — it might be anything. Whatever it is, it is something that will strike at the heart of the country, and it has been planned for years — I have evidence of that.'

'It is typically Teutonic,' murmured Mr. Buncle. 'Well, Mr. Dene, it has got to be stopped, and I am prepared to do all in my power to help. I shall be only too pleased to go back into harness again under your orders.'

'That's the trouble,' said Dene. He got up and began to pace restlessly about the room. 'I can't give any orders because I don't know where to start. If only I could think of some probable meaning for the 'toothpaste' end of it. I've racked my brains until my head aches, but I cannot see how it comes in.'

'It is fairly obvious that X.1 proposes to use 'toothpaste' in some way as a signal to start the whole thing off,' said Mr. Buncle, and Dene made an impatient gesture.

'That,' he snapped shortly, 'is the only obvious thing. But how?'

Mr. Buncle sighed, and deposited the ash from his cigarette carefully in his saucer.

'I'm afraid I can offer no suggestions,' he said apologetically.

Dene made no reply, but stopped in his perambulation of the room and stared moodily out of the window. Mr. Buncle, smoking delicately, sat in unhappy silence, his big brown eyes fixed on his friend's back.

Presently Dene turned. In the warm, clear sunlight his face looked worn and haggard.

'Can I use your telephone?' he inquired. 'There are one or two calls that

I must get through as soon as possible.'

'Of course — of course.' Mr. Buncle rose quickly. 'The telephone is in the small room off the hall. You will be able to speak quite privately. The room is soundproof.'

Dene thanked him and went in search of the instrument. His first call was to an office in Whitehall and occupied him for nearly thirty minutes. Two other calls of shorter duration followed, and when he finally returned to the dining room he found Colgate-Jones and Stacey eating breakfast.

'The Bishop will be dealt with today,' said Dene, and the vicar beamed.

'Good,' he replied. 'I was wondering what was happening in my parish. There will be a tremendous amount of speculation and gossip when they find there was no one at the church this morning to conduct the service. I hope there will only be a mild attack of apoplexy among some of my parishioners.'

'What's the programme for today?' asked Stacey, helping himself to a slice of toast.

'I can't tell you anything definite yet,' answered Dene. 'I haven't made up my mind.'

'Speaking for myself,' remarked Colgate-Jones, 'I may say that I am ready for anything. I've had a good night's rest, an excellent bath, and a most satisfying breakfast, and nothing can dismay me.'

'I'm glad you feel so cheerful,' grunted Dene. 'It's a great deal more than I do.'

The jovial face of the vicar became suddenly grave.

'I realize exactly how you feel,' he replied seriously. 'I haven't lost sight of the urgency of this business.'

'I know you haven't,' said Dene quickly. 'I'm sorry, but this feeling of utter helplessness is getting me a little rattled.' He pulled out his case and helped himself to a cigarette. 'If I could think of something — anything — we could do, it wouldn't be so bad. It's this forced inactivity, when we know that every minute is precious, that's getting me down.'

He dipped the end of his cigarette in the flame of his lighter and puffed jerkily.

Colgate-Jones had opened his mouth to reply when Carol came in. She was wearing an old bathrobe, but otherwise looked neat and clean, though there was a large, ugly bruise partly visible on her forehead.

'Good morning, everybody,' she greeted brightly. 'I hope you haven't eaten all the breakfast, Kupie, I'm starving.'

'Where did you get that thing?' asked the vicar, eyeing the bathrobe critically.

'My Paris model?' said the girl, glancing down at it. 'I found it hanging up behind the door in my room. It may not be very elegant, but I can assure you it's very necessary. What was left of my frock fell to pieces when I took it off.'

'That's one of the things we shall have to see to at once,' remarked Dene. 'We all of us look like scarecrows. If you will hop up to Town this afternoon, Buncle, to an address I will give you, you can bring some clothes back for all of us. We dare not try to get hold of any of our own in case a watch has been set.'

'I'll go immediately after lunch,' said Mr. Buncle, and hurried away to get

175

Carol some breakfast.

'Well, if I can get something to wear I shall feel a bit more human,' said the girl, sitting down in the chair which Stacey pulled up to the table. 'How's everybody? Except for a sore head I feel fine.'

'We might be a great deal worse,' declared her uncle, 'considering what we've been through.'

Carol looked at Dene's troubled face.

'How do we progress?' she asked quietly.

He shook his head.

'We don't,' he answered.

'Well,' she continued practically, 'we've got to do something.'

'There's only one thing we can do that will do any good,' said Dene, 'and that is, find X.1 and stop him giving the signal.'

'Isn't there anything at 'The Flaming Dawn' that would help?' suggested Carol. 'We know somebody there must be connected with X.1.'

'I'm having that looked after,' said Dene. 'I've already been on to the police and arranged with them to watch the place and question Pellissi. I'm doubtful whether it will do much good, though.'

'Why not?' asked Stacey.

'Because I don't suppose for an instant that they'll find out anything,' answered Dene. 'You can take it from me that the whole thing has been too carefully planned.'

'But, hang it all, sir,' protested Stacey, 'they must find *something*. Pellissi *must* be mixed up in this business. Surely he can be *made* to talk.'

'Do you imagine for a second that he knows anything?' retorted Dene. 'Because I'm willing to bet my last shilling that he doesn't. Or any of the other small fry that are working for X.1. You ought to know the German mentality by now, Stacey. I don't suppose that more than half a dozen people *do* know the details of the plot.'

'Couldn't Pellissi be one of the half-dozen?' asked Carol.

'He could, but how are we to know it?' said Dene. 'He's only got to deny all knowledge of anything and how are we going to prove that he's lying? As I say, he may be quite truthful.'

'We were kidnapped from the place — '
began Colgate-Jones.

'Yes,' interrupted Dene, 'but can any of
us say that Pellissi had anything to do
with it? No. All sorts of people frequent a
place like 'The Flaming Dawn'. Any one
of them could have tampered with the
lights and Pellissi be none the wiser.'

They looked at him in silence. There
was so much truth in what he said that
they could not refute it.

'It looks pretty hopeless.' muttered
Stacey.

'It hasn't got to be,' declared Carol
vehemently. 'It *can't* be. There *must* be a
way of finding out if we only think hard
enough.'

Mr. Buncle came back with a tray and
set it down on the table.

'I've been turning this affair over in my
mind,' he said diffidently, as he poured
Carol out a cup of tea, 'and I have a
suggestion to make, if you will allow me.'

'Good Lord, man, go ahead,' said
Dene, and Mr. Buncle bowed his
acknowledgment of the permission.

'The most urgent element in this

matter is the time factor,' he said, speaking slowly and deliberately in his high-pitched voice, 'and that does not allow of anything in the nature of finesse. Whatever is done must be done quickly, and therefore methods that might be advantageous in more leisurely circumstances are likely in this particular case to prove more of a liability than an asset.'

'What exactly do you mean?' asked Dene as Mr. Buncle paused to take breath.

'I mean,' went on Mr. Buncle, 'and I do sincerely hope that you will forgive me for this seeming criticism. I assure you that I have only the thought of our ultimate success at heart . . .'

'Yes, yes, man,' broke in Dene impatiently, 'never mind apologizing for anything. Go on!'

'Well, then,' said Mr. Buncle, looking from one to the other, 'in my humble opinion you have been just a little too clever.'

'Clever?' echoed Michael Dene. 'How?'

'No doubt,' went on Mr. Buncle, 'the opportunity seemed too good a one to

179

miss, but it really has only succeeded, if you look at the position clearly and practically, in blocking up every possible avenue for reaching X.1.'

'What are you getting at?' demanded Dene. 'It may seem quite clear to you, but I haven't the least idea what you are talking about.'

Mr. Buncle's large brown eyes expressed surprise.

'Dear me,' he remarked, 'is it possible that you haven't grasped the point? I am referring to your having decided to allow everyone to be under the impression that you and your friends perished in that house that was bombed.'

'I see what you mean,' said Carol, who had been listening so intently that her breakfast had got cold. 'You mean that by allowing X.1 to think that we died in the raid, we have removed the one possible bait that would draw him?'

Mr. Buncle's face broke into a curious grimace that Carol concluded was his way of smiling.

'Exactly,' he said. 'That is exactly what I was trying to convey. If X.1 was under the impression that you were still alive you would be a source of danger to the success of this plan, whatever it is. His immediate reaction to this would be to try and eliminate that danger. To carry this out he would have to come into the open in some way either personally or by proxy . . .'

Dene's right fist smashed into the palm of his left hand with a sound like the cracking of a whip. It so startled Mr. Buncle that he jumped perceptibly.

'You're right, Buncle!' he cried. 'You're perfectly right. It seemed such a chance at the time that I never really weighed up the result, but you are quite right. Our one and best chance to find X.1 quickly is to offer ourselves as bait to draw him out of his lair.'

Mr. Buncle gave a deprecating but rather gratified cough.

'I think it will have the desired effect,' he said.

15

Towards morning Janice Gould slept heavily, and it was the sound of a key in the lock of the door that wakened her. She sat up in bed, her sleep-hazy brain taking some seconds to grasp the reason for her unfamiliar surroundings and the man who, wearing a beaming smile on his fat and unshaven face, stood at her bedside with a laden tray.

'Good morning,' said Pellissi, and if anyone had doubted his origin, the way in which he held the tray would have dispelled further conjecture. 'I hope you have had a pleasant night. The bed was comfortable, eh? You were warm enough? That is good. See, I have brought you a delicious breakfast. Wheat flakes, an egg, and wafer toast — a breakfast fit for a princess.' He chuckled throatily as he set the tray deftly across her knees. 'Many a princess would have to go without an egg for her breakfast in these days, eh? But to Pellissi nothing is impossible.'

He appeared to be in a high good-humour, but for all that she distrusted him. The fat, flabby face was wreathed in smiles, but the eyes were hard and cruel.

She was grateful for the meal though, especially the tea, and said so.

'Everything that can be done to make your stay comfortable shall be done,' said Pellissi. 'It is just ten-fifteen and a glorious morning. There is a little bell-push over your head. When you have had your breakfast and wish to get up, ring and Anitra will show you to the bathroom. Here are some cigarettes — I had almost forgotten — and you would no doubt like some books to read. I will bring you some.'

'How long do you intend to keep me here?' asked Janice as she cracked the shell of her egg.

'Two days — t'ree — perhaps more.' Pellissi spread out a pair of fat hands and hunched his shoulders. 'It depends . . . '

'On what?' she asked as he paused.

'On circumstances,' he replied vaguely, and before she could ask any more questions had sidled to the door and was gone, locking it after him.

Janice enjoyed her breakfast and the cigarette which followed it. Deliberately she made her mind a blank, refusing admittance to the unpleasant thoughts which clamoured for attention. The dull ache was still at her heart, the leaden weight in the pit of her stomach, and the tears were very near behind her eyes, but resolutely she refused to give way to brooding. Jim Clavering was dead and nothing she could do or say would bring him back. But she could punish the people who had been responsible for his death, and she vowed that she would never rest until she had sought them out and kept her vow. She was convinced that Anitra and Pellissi were mixed up in it, and she wondered just what her best course would be to find out exactly how deeply. She did not believe that they were the chief people concerned, but she hoped that through them she might learn who these people were. She wondered what Michael Dene was doing and what he had thought when she had not returned. Or had the plot, which she had overheard, succeeded? Had Dene and his friends been spirited away during the few moments of darkness when the lights went out to some unknown destination, or even worse? She lit another cigarette, and lying back against the pillows, stared at the slowly wreathing smoke as it trailed spirally ceilingwards. She had almost smoked it to the end when she heard a light footstep outside, the key turned in the lock, and Anitra came in. She was dressed in a housefrock of wine-coloured velvet, which clung closely to her figure until just below the hips and then flared into a wide skirt. Janice had to admit to herself that it enhanced Anitra's dark beauty. She stood on the threshold of the room and surveyed the girl in the bed for a second or two without speaking. Her face was expressionless; for all the emotion it displayed she might have been made of wax. Then she advanced to the foot of the bed.

'I've come to have a little talk with you,'

she said abruptly. 'I hope that a night's sleep has made you more reasonable.'

'In what way?' asked Janice.

'I'm hoping that you are prepared to tell me who sent you to pry into things that don't concern you at 'The Flaming Dawn',' said Anitra.

Janice smiled.

'I don't see how a night's sleep could endow me with such a vivid imagination as that,' she retorted. 'I've already told you that I haven't the remotest idea what you are talking about.'

Anitra's face hardened.

'So you still intend to be stubborn,' she said. 'Well . . . '

'It isn't a case of being stubborn,' interrupted Janice. 'It's merely that I refuse to concoct a story to satisfy your distorted idea of what you think to be the truth.'

'It's quite useless lying . . . ' began Anitra, and again Janice interrupted her.

'I'm not lying,' she said curtly. 'You are either completely crazy or else you have such a guilty conscience that the most innocent action appears to you to have some deep design directed against you . . . '

'Stop pretending!' snapped Anitra. 'You were spying at 'The Flaming Dawn', and it's no use pretending that you weren't. It's no use, either, trying to kid me that you were acting on your own. Somebody sent you. I want to know who it was, and I'm going to know.'

Her whole attitude was menacing as she leaned forward across the foot of the bed and stared at Janice through narrowed eyes.

Janice returned her stare without flinching.

'I'm sorry,' she replied coolly, 'I was never any good at making up stories — particularly fairytales. I've told you the truth, and if you don't choose to believe me — well, that's your business . . . '

'You'll find that it's your business, too,' said Anitra between her teeth. 'I'll give you until tonight to think it over, and then I shall come back and try what a little gentle persuasion will do. It won't be so gentle, either!'

She swung out of the room, her face convulsed with fury, slammed the door and turned the key.

Janice heard the dull thudding of her high-heeled shoes fade away along the carpeted corridor, and settled herself more comfortably in bed. The prospect, if Anitra carried out her threat, was not a very pleasant one. There was nothing, however, that she could do about it and it was useless worrying. As likely as not the woman had merely been trying to frighten her, and meanwhile there was still the greater part of the day to be got through somehow. If Pellissi brought the books he had promised it would help. At least it would do something to break the monotony and keep her from thinking — an unprofitable occupation since her thoughts revolved in a perpetual circle.

The rest of the morning wore slowly away, but Pellissi did not bring the books or anything else. At three o'clock she began to feel hungry and rang the bell over her bed, but nobody answered it. There was no sound at all in the house, and she came to the conclusion that there was nobody in. She fell into a doze, and when she awoke it was five o'clock. She felt ravenous and thirsty, but a repeated onslaught on the bell produced no results. She got up and looked out of the window. It was a fine evening, but all she could see were trees and a patch of garden. She put on her clothes, sat down on the side of the bed and lit a cigarette. She was feeling bored and depressed, and her head ached dully. She finished her cigarette, stubbed out the end in an ashtray on the bedside table, and getting up, rambled about the small room. Her hunger began to get worse, and she would have given almost anything for a cup of tea. She tried the door in the faint hope that it was unlocked, but it was fast. She could see the end of the key projecting from the lock, and a half-forgotten memory came to her — the memory of an incident in a book she had once read. The detective in the story had escaped from a locked room by doing something with a sheet of newspaper and the key. How? She frowned in an effort to recall the situation, and then, as the details came back to her, her face cleared. That was it. He had pushed a sheet of paper under the door and pushed the key out of the lock. It had fallen on the paper and he had pulled the sheet and the key back under the door. If she could do the same . . .

She bent down. There was space enough under the door, but she had no paper. A thought struck her and she went quickly over to a tallboy in the corner. Opening a drawer, she pushed aside the oddments it contained and found, as she had hoped, that the drawer was lined with newspaper. Pulling it out she went back to the door, and spreading the sheet of newspaper on the floor, pushed it carefully under the door until more than two-thirds of it was in the passage outside. When this was done she turned her attention to the key. Very little of it protruded into the room, and when she tried to twist it with her fingers so as to bring the wards in line with the slot, it refused to budge. Again and again she tried, until her fingers were sore, but without result. There was not enough she could grip. With a pair of pliers it would have been easy, but with only her fingers

. . . And then she remembered that in her bag was a pair of eyebrow pluckers. They *might* do the trick. She found them after an eager search and tried them on the key.

It was some time before she succeeded in her endeavour, but eventually the key turned slowly. She stooped and peered through the keyhole until she saw the wards come down and block it up, and then she straightened up with a little sighing expulsion of breath. Now, if she pushed gently, the key should fall out on to the paper . . . She tried the experiment and heard the key drop with a dull little thud. Had it fallen on the spread newspaper or had it overshot the mark?

With infinite care she pulled the newspaper slowly back under the door and the key came with it. She had been successful. In another minute she had twisted it in the lock and the door was open!

She stood for a moment in the passage outside listening, but the house was still silent, and she tiptoed to the staircase. Here she listened again, but no sound reached her and she began to descend. Her heart was thumping. She was free — could, if she liked, open the front door and walk quietly away. Perhaps that would be the best thing to do and go to the police. Her original intention of finding out for herself who had been responsible for Jim Clavering's death, looked like proving a fiasco. She might stay here for ever and never learn anything more than she knew at present. And that was enough to set the police working . . .

She crossed the hall and her hand was on the front door latch when she heard the sound of an approaching car and paused. It came nearer and stopped outside the house. Anitra's voice called to someone to 'hurry up', and Janice heard the sound of rapid footsteps on gravel. It was too late to attempt to leave now. She looked hastily round her for a hiding place, saw a door, and hurrying over to it, pulled it open. It was a cupboard for coats and hats, and slipping inside she drew the door shut just as a key scraped in the lock and the front door opened.

16

Sunday — 1.45 p.m.

Mr. Horace Smith, who was known to the Third Reich as Y.3, wiped his lips, carefully folded his napkin, and looked up at the elderly woman who had just brought in his coffee.

'An excellent luncheon, Mrs. Ruddle,' he remarked. 'Considering these difficult times of rationing you have managed remarkably well.'

The woman smiled.

'The butcher let me have a larger joint than usual, sir,' she said, 'a nice bit of beef. It's a pleasant change from this everlasting mutton.'

'It is, indeed,' declared Mr. Smith, draining his cup of black coffee and rising to his feet, 'a very nice and tender piece of beef, too, and cooked perfectly.'

A very pleasant gentleman to work for, thought Mrs. Ruddle as she cleared away the dishes. Always ready with a word of praise for anything that pleased and never given to grumbling. It was a pity Ruddle wasn't more like him; always finding fault with his food, as if it was her fault there was a war on and things were difficult to get. Maybe he was tired working all them hours at the factory, but that was no excuse to get bad-tempered.

'The pleasant gentleman's' thoughts would at that moment have astounded the simple-minded Mrs. Ruddle had she been aware of them, for he was standing at the window of the comfortably furnished lounge gazing out across the well-kept lawn and meditating on the fact that another week would see the downfall of this country in which he had lived for so long and which he hated with all the strength of his being. Several newspapers lay beside his chair and they all contained references to the impending 'Second Front', and the devastation that had been caused in Germany by the hoards of British and American bombers that were so relentlessly raining down their messengers of destruction. There were complacent conjectures as to how long Germany would stand the strain of continuous bombing and speculations as to the strength of the Luftwaffe.

Mr. Smith's genial face hardened for a moment. Did the fools really think that Germany was anything like finished? Did they imagine for a single instant that she was playing this waiting game because she could not retaliate? If they did, in seven days' time they would get a very rude awakening. The devastation that Germany had suffered would be nothing compared to what was coming to this conceited and bumptious people who considered that they had been created to rule the world. That dream of a 'Second Front' and eventual victory was destined to fade into nothing like any other illusion, leaving a reality of chaos and destruction in its place that would teach these upstarts once and for all who was the master race.

Mr. Smith felt a sudden patriotic and fanatical glow irradiate his whole being as he remembered that *he* had been chosen as one of the people to help bring about that wonderful result. He and his small band of colleagues, working under the leadership of X.1, had devoted years to perfecting the plan, and the moment was almost at hand when their labours would bear full fruit. The waiting had been long and difficult. It required a patience and a nerve that was almost superhuman to hold back while Germany suffered reverse after reverse — to refrain from prematurely playing the trump card and losing the game.

Mr. Smith turned away from the window, helped himself to a cigar from a box beside his chair, and sat down with a contented sigh. The danger which for a moment had threatened to upset the whole scheme and render all the careful preparation futile, had been discovered and dealt with in time. This was due to the genius of the unknown X.1. How he had found out that Clavering had stumbled on the secret was a mystery to Mr. Smith. But then everything concerning X.1 was a mystery. He directed operations but remained himself invisible and unknown. The carefully coded messages which reached Mr. Smith at his office originated out of the blue, but he acted upon them without question.

He had finished his cigar and was dozing when the gloomy Mr. Jenkins arrived.

'Come in,' said Mr. Smith genially. 'Come in, my dear fellow.' He shut the front door behind the visitor and escorted him back to the lounge. 'Well, did you confirm that report from Arost?'

Mr. Jenkins, who was known to the Third Reich as Y.4, nodded.

'The bomb killed everybody in the house,' he said. 'It fell in the garden a few yards away and there is scarcely a brick standing. I've seen the place and had a chat to one of the N.F.S. men. The house is just a heap of smoking ruins and nobody was saved.'

Mr. Smith rubbed his fat hands with quick pleasure.

'Well, that's that,' he remarked cheerfully. 'The — er — incident which might have proved disastrous is now closed.'

Mr. Jenkins settled himself in an easy-chair and accepted the cigar which was offered him.

'It's a great relief,' he grunted, 'and not only that, it has got rid of a very dangerous and clever man.'

'Meaning Dene?' inquired Mr. Smith.

Mr. Jenkins nodded.

'Meaning Dene,' he replied, carefully lighting his cigar. 'That man knew a great deal, Smith. Here.' He tapped his forehead with a bony forefinger. 'He will be difficult to replace.'

'His replacement will not be necessary.' Mr. Smith beamed across at his companion. 'These British will not require a Special Branch after next week.'

'I hope you may be right,' said Mr. Jenkins slowly and thoughtfully. His tone was so serious that Mr. Smith stared at him, the smile vanishing from his flabby face.

'What do you mean?' he asked quickly. 'You don't imagine that anything can go wrong?'

'I don't know what I imagine,' grunted Mr. Jenkins. 'I have a queer sort of foreboding . . . '

'Nonsense!' broke in Mr. Smith sharply. 'It's the reaction, that's all. Just nerves, Jenkins, nothing more. You must pull out of it.'

The taciturn Mr. Jenkins examined the glowing end of his cigar.

'You are probably quite right,' he said after a pause. 'I expect my nerves *are* pretty strained — I think we've all felt a sense of strain for a long time.'

'You must not let it get the better of you,' said Mr. Smith. 'You are not on fireguard tonight, are you?'

Mr. Jenkins shook his head.

'Then,' went on Mr. Smith, 'if you take my advice you will go to bed early and have a good rest. Nothing can possibly go wrong. X.1 has foreseen everything down to the last detail. There will be no hitch.'

Mr. Jenkins said nothing, but his gloomy expression remained, and Mr. Smith eyed him apprehensively. Was Jenkins' nerve going? he asked himself. If so, he would have to suffer short shrift. In that organization they could not afford to have anyone who might crack under the strain. He made up his mind to mention the matter in his next report to X.1. There had been a man once who had cracked . . . The coroner had brought in a verdict of accidental death, but Mr.

Smith knew how that man had died.

He allowed nothing of his thoughts to appear in his face, which wore its usual expression of good-nature, and chatted to Mr. Jenkins about a number of subjects.

'Is Hanson coming in tonight?' asked Mr. Jenkins, breaking suddenly into the middle of an account by Mr. Smith of a golf match he had played the previous week.

'Hanson — yes, he may drop in,' said Mr. Smith. 'Well, as I was telling you, we reached the seventh green . . . '

He concluded his anecdote and related another, and presently Mr. Jenkins began to shed a little of his gloom. It grew dark outside and Mr. Smith got up, drew the curtains over the windows and switched on the light. He produced a chess-board and men, a siphon of soda, glasses, and a bottle of Johnnie Walker, and the two men settled down to play chess. They looked the epitome of two middle-aged business men spending a quiet Sunday evening, and no one would have dreamed for a single instant that they were other than what they seemed. Mr. Smith was very well known among the residents of the little housing estate where he lived, and very well liked, for he was always jovial and had a pleasant word for everybody. His neighbours would have been aghast if they had even suspected what really lay beneath that genial and pleasant exterior.

They finished their game, which Mr. Smith won, and began another. Halfway through this, when it looked as though Mr. Jenkins had forced his opponent into a particularly tight corner, they were interrupted by the ringing of the front door bell.

With an exclamation of annoyance Mr. Smith got up, excused himself, and went out to see who was the disturber of their peace.

It was Hanson.

'Oh, it's you,' said Mr. Smith as the other limped into the hall. 'I was wondering if you'd come round.'

'Anybody here?' asked Hanson quickly.

'Only Jenkins,' answered Mr. Smith. 'We're playing chess . . . '

'I came to talk to you — both of you,' interrupted Hanson. 'It's urgent.'

He limped into the lounge and Mr. Smith followed a little anxiously.

'Well, what is it?' he demanded as he shut the door.

'I've just left Trigford,' said Hanson abruptly. 'He and Altman were at 'The Flaming Dawn' this evening. Dene's there.'

Mr. Jenkins uttered an exclamation and Mr. Smith's eyebrows rose in half circles high on his domed forehead.

'Dene?' he echoed. 'Impossible. Michael Dene and his associates were killed by one of our bombs during the raid last night . . . '

'Were they?' snapped Hanson. 'Well, either Dene's got a double or it's his ghost that Trigford saw at 'The Flaming Dawn' half an hour ago.'

17

Sunday — 10.15 p.m.

Michael Dene let his eyes rove disparagingly round 'The Flaming Dawn' and brought them back to the face of his companion with a slight shrug of the shoulders.

'Well, here we are,' he remarked, 'and I hope that we shan't be wasting our time.'

Frank Stacey signalled to a waiter and ordered a bottle of Johnnie Walker.

'Yes, sir. Your name please, sir,' said the man.

Stacey give his name and the man hurried away.

'I've got a feeling we shall have some luck,' said Stacey, when the waiter had gone. 'Most of the people who were here last night are here again tonight. That fellow over by the band platform, near the drummer. I'll swear he was one of the men who were watching us last night.'

Dene's eyes travelled eagerly round the place.

'H'm,' he muttered, 'I see the chap you mean. He's seen us, too.'

The man Stacey had referred to was a thin, dark individual. He had been talking to the drummer and as he turned round he had looked straight across at their table, which was the same one they had occupied on the previous night. Just for a second there was a flicker of recognition in his eyes and then his gaze passed on. After a moment he strolled leisurely towards a table on the other side of the dance-floor and joined a group who were seated at it. They consisted of two men and a girl. The girl was very smartly dressed and heavily made up. Her fair hair was the colour of maize and she wore it dressed high. She was smoking a cigarette through a long scarlet holder, the same colour as her lips and nails. The men with her were middle-aged. They looked like city men. All three were drinking whisky and ginger ale.

The thin man sat down and one of the others poured him out a drink. He said something and they all laughed, but none of them so much as glanced in Dene and Stacey's direction.

Stacey's waiter came back with a bottle and siphon and glasses. The bottle of Johnnie Walker was ostentatiously labelled with Stacey's name. It was a polite fiction at 'The Flaming Dawn' that members bought stocks of drinks and kept them there to be served up when they were required. The waiter whisked the table with a napkin, set down bottle, siphon, and glasses, and bowed himself away.

Stacey opened the bottle and poured out two drinks.

'Well,' he said, 'I hope the fish will rise to the bait.'

'And now you know what the bait feels like,' said Dene with a twinkle in his eye.

They drank, lit cigarettes, and settled back to keep a watchful eye on what was going on around them and to await developments.

Dene had acted on Mr. Buncle's suggestion, after a conference with the others, and 'The Flaming Dawn' had been decided upon as a good place to use as a hook. It was used by the group controlled by X.1 — they had plenty of evidence to prove that — and the appearance of Michael Dene, alive and well, was almost sure to start something. It had been necessary to take Stacey along with him, for without the company of a member he would not have been admitted to the place. Carol had told them that the management were very strict on this point, an assertion that Stacey had emphatically backed up, though Dene was rather under the impression that it was because he didn't want to be left out of it than anything else. Colgate-Jones and Carol had been very disappointed that they were not allowed to come along too, but Dene, in this, had been adamant, refusing to listen to all arguments or cajolery. It was, he knew, a dangerous business they were engaged on, and although this was not an argument that was likely to carry much weight with either the vicar or the girl, he had no intention of placing them in more danger than he could help.

A telephone message to London had

brought down that afternoon to Mr. Buncle's little cottage three thoroughly experienced members of the Special Branch, and to these men Dene had explained the whole situation and given minute instructions. Their job was to trail the trailers. By exposing himself in the open Dene hoped to draw the Nazi group's attentions to him, and these three men, by keeping a constant observation on him, would be able to discover just who these people were, and possibly be led at length to X.1 himself. That was Dene's greatest objective, for the finding of X.1 in time would effectually put a stop to the plot he had hatched being carried out, since it was fairly obvious that nothing would happen until he gave the signal. If he could be prevented from doing this, then nothing would happen at all, and the whole scheme would fizzle out. After June 21st it would be too late. This applied to both sides, and it was this time factor that worried Dene so intensely. Nobody knew better than he the danger he was exposing himself to. X.1's main object, as soon as he was aware that Dene had survived the bomb, would be to kill him and his associates, and in his desperation it was quite likely that he would throw finesse to the winds and make an open attack. Dene was aware and prepared for this. He was quite willing to sacrifice himself if the worst came to the worst, provided that his sacrifice was not in vain, but led to the discovery of the heads of the group and the shattering of their plan. For this reason an elaborate system of signals had been devised so that he would notify his men of any circumstance, or any person, that appeared to him to be suspicious.

They had not been able to follow Stacey and he into 'The Flaming Dawn', but they were not far away and at least within call in case of trouble — always supposing that there was time to call them. Dene did not expect that anything would happen inside 'The Flaming Dawn'. It was hardly likely that the same trick would be attempted twice, but he was well on his guard. If the lights should suddenly fail again, he was prepared.

The band finished a quick-step and,

heralded by the usual roll on the drum, Pellissi came forward to make his announcement. The lights dimmed, a spot focussed on the curtains at the back of the band dais, and Anitra appeared.

Tonight she was dressed in a tight-fitting frock of emerald green velvet cut daringly low. Her hair was caught back on one side with a ribbon of the same colour as her dress, and she wore elbow-length gloves of emerald green kid. While the band played the introduction to her opening number she surveyed her audience with her usual lazy, half-insolent expression, and then, stepping down to the microphone at exactly the right moment, began to sing.

She sang three numbers — different numbers to the ones she had used on the Saturday — bowed slightly to acknowledge the applause, and disappeared behind the falling curtains.

'It beats me,' said Stacey, refilling their glasses as the lights came up, 'why a woman like that wastes her time in this place. She could get a huge salary on the halls.'

Dene lit a cigarette.

'Maybe she has a good reason for preferring 'The Flaming Dawn',' he remarked, 'or perhaps Pellissi has got her bound down under contract.'

'I should think that was the more likely,' said Stacey. 'Nasty bit of work, Pellissi. Do you think he's got anything to do with this group?'

Dene shrugged his shoulders.

'It's impossible to say who has and who hasn't,' he replied. 'That's what we're here to find out.'

He looked casually across at the table where the fair-haired girl was talking rapidly and animatedly to the dark thin man. He and the other two men were listening attentively. They were, apparently, completely oblivious of the presence of Dene and Stacey, but for some reason or other Dene was convinced that this was only a piece of camouflage. An instinct told him that they were all four very much aware of his presence indeed.

'I wonder what happened to Janice Gould?' said Stacey suddenly. 'She's not here tonight.'

Dene flicked the ash off his cigarette into an ashtray.

'You didn't expect she would be, did you?' he answered gravely. 'I'm very much afraid that we shall not see Miss Gould again — not alive, at any rate. Somehow or other they got wind of the fact that she was in possession of that letter and acted accordingly.'

Stacey swallowed half the contents of his glass abruptly.

'It's a horrible thought,' he muttered. 'A young girl . . . '

'That wouldn't worry them,' said Dene. 'Young or old, male or female — it would be all the same to X.1 if his plans were in danger of being upset.'

The fair girl had paused in her flood of speech and her companions were laughing heartily. She pressed the stub of her cigarette out of the scarlet holder on the edge of the ashtray, said something, and rose to her feet. The others got up while she left the table and then sat down again as she made her way across the dance floor to the door that gave admittance to the cloakroom.

As she disappeared from view the band started a foxtrot, and a few couples began to dance. They partially obscured Dene's view of the three men at the table, and when he got a clear sight of them again he saw that the thin dark man had vanished. He looked all round the place, but there was no sign of him anywhere.

'Did you see what happened to our dark friend?' he asked Stacey, and received a shake of the head in reply.

'No,' said Stacey. 'The dancers were in the way.'

'Same here,' said Dene. 'But it was only for a moment. He must have been pretty slippy to have disappeared in such a short time.'

'Where can he have gone?' muttered Stacey, with a frown. 'There's no exit over that side. If he'd gone to any of the exits on the other we should have seen him.'

At that moment they did see him. There was a square pillar near their table supporting one of the arches to the alcoves which lined the walls, and the dark thin man suddenly appeared from behind this and came towards them. He

212

passed close to the table with scarcely a glance at them, but when he was abreast he flicked a little screw of paper on to the cloth in front of them. It was done so deftly that nobody could have seen it, and he was gone and had passed through the curtained archway to the vestibule before the small, rolled-up paper had come to rest.

Dene, thoroughly astonished at this unexpected development, though his face remained impassive, pretended to stub out his cigarette in the ashtray, and palmed the message, if that was what it was.

'I'm going to the lavatory,' he said to Stacey. 'I shan't be long, but mind your P's and Q's while I'm gone.'

He got up and strolled leisurely towards the door leading to the gentlemen's cloakroom. The lavatory was empty, and quickly unrolling the scrap of paper he glanced at it. It was part of an envelope, and scribbled across it in pencil was the following:

'*You are being watched. Be careful. The stout man in grey, I think.*'

That was all. There was no signature.

Dene frowned at the message, utterly and completely puzzled. Who was the thin dark man and what had prompted this warning? Was it genuine, or some sort of a trap — a deliberate attempt to direct his suspicions on to the wrong person. He knew who was referred to by the 'stout man in grey'. He had been there when they had arrived — a round, red-faced man with fair hair, middle-aged, and possessing the appearance of a prosperous tradesman. He was in the company of a good-looking girl in A.T.S. uniform, and Dene had concluded that he was her uncle or some kind of relation.

He made his way back inside 'The Flaming Dawn' puzzled and wondering, and here he received a second and even greater surprise. Their table was empty.

Stacey had disappeared!

18

Sunday — 11.40 p.m.

Janice crouched back in the narrow confines of the cupboard, and her heart thumped so loudly that she was certain that it must be heard by the people who had come in.

'We haven't got very long,' she heard Anitra say, followed by the closing of the front door. 'Pellissi will miss me if I don't get back to 'The Flaming Dawn' by a quarter to one. Until then he'll be busy checking the new consignment.'

'I don't know that we ought . . . ' began the deep tones of a man's voice.

'We've got to!' Anitra interrupted vehemently. 'I tell you that if this is left to Pellissi we shall find ourselves in the dock — all of us. He's suddenly developed a conscience or something and become as yellow as a prairie dog. We've got to take this matter into our own hands.'

'What do you suggest?' asked the other. 'I'll admit that if this girl was snooping on us it's a pretty serious matter . . . '

'She was — you can take my word for that,' snapped Anitra. 'And if we let her go — which is that fool Pellissi's idea — she'll report at once to the authorities. You know what that'll mean?'

'I realize that,' said the man, 'but you can't keep her a prisoner here indefinitely . . . '

'I'm not suggesting that she should be kept a prisoner *anywhere*,' broke in Anitra, and there was a significance in her voice that made Janice's blood run cold.

'Good God, you don't mean that we should — that she should . . . ' The man's tone was aghast and he stammered helplessly.

'Why not?' said Anitra calmly. 'It means our safety, doesn't it? It means either that or the ruining of all our plans. Why be squeamish, Levistien?'

'I'm not squeamish, but surely there's some other way?' muttered her companion.

'There's no other way and you know it,' retorted Anitra. 'Both you and Pellissi know it, but neither of you has got the guts to admit it.'

'Oh, I say, come, Anitra . . . ' began the man angrily.

'It's true and you know it,' said Anitra curtly. 'Neither of you will face the situation with bare hands. You both want to handle it with kid gloves. Well, that would be your affair if you two were the only ones involved. But I'm in this, too, and I don't propose to suffer for your Sunday schoolish qualms.'

'If it's likely to be as serious as you say,' said her companion dubiously after a pause, 'then I suppose you're right, m'dear. But if this girl has been spying on us she won't have been acting on her own. Whatever she's learned she'll have passed back to the people who are employing her . . . '

'I don't think she's learned anything definite,' said Anitra, 'but I think she was on the point of learning it when I discovered her. Since then she hasn't had a chance of passing anything to anyone. However, whatever her suspicions were before, she knows now that she was right, and the moment she's allowed to go free we shall all be arrested.'

'Yes, that's true. You're quite right, Anitra.' The man called Levistien's voice was more decided. 'It's a nasty business, but I see that it will have to be gone through.'

'That's the first sensible thing I've heard for a long time,' remarked Anitra coolly.

'You say this girl refuses to admit anything or to talk?' asked the other.

'She's playing the innocent,' said Anitra, 'and it nearly worked with Pellissi. He wouldn't have been so easily hoodwinked if she'd been a man, but she's a girl and pretty, so Pellissi endowed her with all the virtues. She won't talk by being asked nicely, but under a little persuasion she'll say a mouthful. You mark my words.'

'This thing has got to be handled carefully,' muttered Levistien, and Janice could almost see the frown of concentration with which he spoke. 'We'll have to find out just who's behind her and how much they know or suspect. After that we can decide what to do.'

'Come upstairs and see her now,' said Anitra. 'I'll do the questioning and you can do the persuading. We ought to have the whole story out of her in half an hour. She doesn't look the sort who could bear much physical pain.'

Janice heard her move over to the staircase with a thrill of horror. It would only take them a few seconds to discover that she was no longer locked in that room . . .

'Just a minute,' said Levistien, 'what can I do to her?'

'Burn her with a cigarette,' answered Anitra as calmly as though she were remarking that it was a nice evening. 'If you do it cleverly it can be very painful indeed. Now come on and don't waste any more time. I want to get to 'The Flaming Dawn'.'

Her high-heeled shoes began to ascend the stairs, and Janice pushed open the door of the cupboard an inch. She could see a flash of emerald green between the white banisters, and the dark cloth of Levistien's trousers as he followed it. Overcoming the sudden panic which made her feel sick, she crept out of the cupboard and ran towards the front door. In her hurry and terror she forgot the highly polished floor and slipped. To save herself from falling she grasped wildly at a chair which slid away from her hand, and she fell heavily with a thud that shook the house.

She was bruised and shaken, and as she scrambled frantically to her feet she heard a startled exclamation from above and the sound of running feet. Ignoring the pain in her left arm, she dashed for the front door and had just succeeded in twisting the lock and pulling it open when Anitra appeared at the top of the stairs with Levistien behind her. Janice heard the woman's shout of rage as she fled into the darkness of the night.

'Stop her!' cried Anitra. 'We must stop her.'

She caught up her long, tight-fitting green dress, and with Levistien at her heels sped down the stairs.

'You go ahead,' she cried. 'You can run faster than me. Go on — hurry! You must catch her.'

He sprinted past her and down the narrow drive. By this time Janice had reached the gate, and his footsteps thudding along behind her leant wings to her feet. She tore out into the road and ran as she had never run before. She had no idea where the road led, and did not care very much. Her one thought was to get away from those pursuing footsteps. But her high heels hampered her, and although she had had a fairly good start they seemed to be getting nearer. It was a very dark night, and she could scarcely see anything at all except that the road was narrow and lined on either side with hedges and trees. She searched frantically for an opening in those seemingly endless hedges, believing that if she could find one she might elude her pursuer. But nothing of the sort presented itself. The pain in her arm was increasing and she was breathing with difficulty. Once she stumbled and almost fell, and in spite of all her efforts the footsteps behind her were steadily growing nearer. The darkness around her became flecked with little pin-points of white light as the blood pounded through her head, and the muscles of her legs ached, but she gritted her teeth and kept on. Nearer ... nearer still came the relentless thudding in her rear. A sharp pain shot through her side suddenly and she found herself gasping for breath. She knew that she would be able to go very little farther — that she was almost spent. The footsteps were not more than six yards behind her now and decreasing the distance with every stride. A helpless feeling of despair came over her. It was no good, she might just as well give up. She was bound to be caught. And then suddenly at her side, appearing out of the blackness like magic, she saw a white gate. She almost flung herself at it and fumbled for the latch. More by luck than anything else her fingers found it and pressed it down. She was through the gate and running like the wind up the path beyond as Levistien reached the gate and paused. Before her was a porch and a door, and she banged on it with her clenched fists, breathing a prayer that the people who lived there would still be up. She heard a movement within and the door opened.

'Please,' she gasped, 'help me . . . ' and fell across the threshold into the arms of the astonished Mr. Buncle.

19

Sunday — Midnight

Levistien, his hand on the gate, both saw and heard. As the door closed, shutting out Janice from his sight, he hesitated, made a tentative movement to open the little gate, thought better of it, and turned reluctantly away. There was nothing he could do at the moment. He had no idea who occupied the cottage — probably friends of the girl. She had made straight for it as though she realized that it spelt sanctuary.

Halfway along the dark road he met Anitra.

'Where's the girl?' she demanded harshly, as she saw that he was alone. 'What have you done with her?'

He explained briefly, and she stamped her foot.

'You fool!' She was almost incoherent with rage. 'Why did you let her get away?

What are we going to do now? We can't just leave things as they are. We've got to get hold of that girl before she can talk . . . '

'Don't be ridiculous,' broke in Levistien impatiently. 'How can we? We can't break in and take her. That would be worse than doing nothing . . . '

'We've got to do something,' snapped Anitra. 'We can't just sit down and say that's that.'

'Have you any idea who lives in the cottage?' asked Levistien, and she shook her head.

'No,' she replied. 'What does it matter . . . ?'

'It matters a lot,' answered Levistien. 'She made straight for the place, and it looks to me as though it's occupied by friends of hers. If that's so I don't like the look of things at all.'

'Oh, you don't?' sneered Anitra. 'You don't like the look of things? Well, why don't you do something about it, then?'

'It's all very well to say that,' protested Levistien angrily, 'but what can I do?'

'You can come back with me to 'The

Flaming Dawn' and see Pellissi,' said Anitra. 'Somebody's got to do something, and quickly, unless we want to find ourselves in gaol.'

'And in the meanwhile supposing the girl leaves — what then?' said Levistien.

Anitra considered this.

'Yes, you're right,' she said, after a moment. 'At least we know where she is now. You'd better stay here and keep watch on the cottage. I'll go back to 'The Flaming Dawn' and tell Pellissi what's happened. If the girl *does* come out don't let her get away again.'

Levistien was not, apparently, enamoured with the arrangement.

'How long shall I have to stop here?' he said dubiously.

'Until I, or someone I send, relieves you,' retorted the woman. 'Now get back to the cottage as quickly as you can.'

She hurried away in the darkness and Levistien retraced his steps.

Anitra reached the bungalow, went in and slipped on her coat, and came quickly out to the car. She backed it with difficulty in the narrow road, turned it, and drove as fast as she dared in the direction of 'The Flaming Dawn'.

She found Pellissi in his office talking to a small, dark, rat-like man who was smoking a large cigar.

'Where have you been?' greeted Pellissi. 'I have looked for you everywhere . . . '

'I've been home,' said Anitra, 'and I've got bad news. The girl has got away.'

'The girl has . . . ' Pellissi echoed her words and half rose from behind his large desk. 'What do you say?'

'You heard,' said Anitra. '*The — girl — has — got — away.*'

'How? How?' Pellissi got up excitedly. 'What fresh lunacy have you been up to?'

'If you keep quiet I'll tell you what happened,' said Anitra, and as Pellissi calmed himself with an effort, proceeded to do so.

'Now see what your meddling has done,' wailed Pellissi when she had finished. 'Why didn't you leave the girl alone in the first place? I told you it was a mistake to take her to the bungalow at all, and you see what has resulted. All our plans will be ruined just because you had to be stupid.'

'Look here, guv'nor,' broke in the rat-faced man, 'it's no good goin' on like that. This is a serious matter, and we're all goin' to be in a serious jam unless we do somethin' . . . '

'You tell me that,' said Pellissi, waving his podgy hands about. 'You tell me it is serious, eh? As if I did not know. Tell me something else. Tell me how we can get out of it. Tell me . . . '

'I'll tell you,' cut in Anitra. 'You can get out of it by getting the girl back at once — before she has time to talk.'

'And that is easy, eh?' Pellissi swung round on her, his fat, greasy face shining with perspiration. 'Get the girl back — just like that,' he snapped his fingers. 'So — that is easy.'

'Of course it's easy,' snapped Anitra. 'Get Tim and Mark and Syd here to take the car and fetch her.'

Pellissi stared at her and then shook his head.

'No, no, I will not do it,' he declared. 'Take her by force, you mean? No, it would be madness.'

'It's madness not to, guv'nor,' broke in Syd. 'It's risky, but it's more risky to leave her where she is. Even if she knows nothin' about anythin' else she's only got to say that you kept her a prisoner at the bungalow and you're for it — we're all for it. It was a mistake to touch 'er in the beginnin', I'll agree, but it 'ud be a bigger mistake not to go after her now.'

Pellissi pulled out a large handkerchief and mopped his wet forehead with a trembling hand.

'If only you'd let well alone and not interfered,' he said huskily. 'See what you've done by your stupidity.'

'Cut it out,' said Anitra. 'If *you'd* done what I wanted you to do in the first place this situation would never have arisen. But you were too white-livered — you're too white-livered now . . . '

'Quit the slanging match,' said Syd, getting up abruptly. 'I'm in this as much as you two, and I'm going to do something about it. Talk won't get us anywhere. I'll rake up Tim and Mark and get goin'.' He turned to Anitra: 'Have you any idea how many people there are in this cottage?' he asked.

She shook her head.

'Oh, well,' he went on. 'Three of us an' Levistien should be able to deal with 'em.' He strode over to the door. 'We'll bring the girl back 'ere,' he said, 'an' you'd better arrange that she doesn't have a chance to get away again.'

'You can leave that to me,' said Anitra.

★ ★ ★

Levistien made his way back to the cottage in which Janice had taken refuge and took up his stand on the opposite side of the road beneath the spreading branches of a large tree. The small house was in complete darkness — not even a glow showed in any of the windows, and either the blackout arrangements were exceptionally good or the inhabitants were using the back rooms.

Levistien was not feeling particularly good-tempered. He was uneasy, and beginning to wish himself well out of the whole business. It was too late, however, to wish that, but he would rather somebody else had been found to attend to this side of it. That was the trouble when you had to work with women. They landed you in all sorts of trouble through acting on impulse without giving any thought to the consequences. If Anitra had taken the trouble to think, all this mess might have been avoided. But Anitra was always impulsive.

He would have liked a cigarette, but decided that it would be too risky. It was lucky that the road was little used, for if anybody saw him lurking here it would look suspicious. It was too late for anyone to believe that he was waiting for a girl. And yet that was, when you came to think of it, exactly what he was doing. Not in the conventional way, of course. He wondered how long it would be before Anitra sent somebody to take his place. It would be an hour or more at the least. She had to explain things to Pellissi first.

He strolled a few yards up the road, turned, and came back. Already he seemed to have been here an age. It was surprising how slowly time went by when you wanted it to pass quickly: and how quickly when you didn't.

The lights of a car appeared dimly in the distance, and presently it passed him, going in the direction of Staines, but that was the only thing that broke the monotony of his vigil. There was no sign of life at all in the cottage. All the inmates might have been in bed and asleep — probably were, he thought disgustedly.

After what seemed hours, another car approached. It was travelling slowly, and when it had passed him it slowed down and stopped. He heard a door open and shut, and presently the sound of footsteps coming towards him. He pressed himself back in the shelter of the tree trunk as they drew nearer, watchfully alert. It might be someone from Anitra and it might not. The person, whoever it was, came close, and a dim shadow went by within a few feet of him. He waited. If it was someone looking for him they would come back. Presently the footsteps stopped, there was a pause, and then they began again. The man was coming back.

Levistien slipped out from his place of concealment and began to stroll towards the walker. A dimmed torch flashed out of the gloom as he drew near, and a voice whispered quickly:

'Is that you, Levistien?'

Levistien recognized the voice and replied at once: 'Hello, Syd. I . . . '

'Where did you get to?' Syd broke in. 'I've been lookin' for you.'

'I didn't know it was you,' answered Levistien. 'I was hidden behind that tree. How was I to know it was you?'

'Well, it doesn't matter now,' said Syd impatiently. 'Look here, Levistien, we've got to get hold of that girl. I've got Tim and Mark in the car, and between the four of us it shouldn't be difficult.'

'Do you mean you're going to take her by force?' demanded Levistien. 'It's going to be very serious if we're found out . . . '

'It's going to be very serious, anyway,' retorted Syd. 'Anitra's got us into this mess, an' we've just got to get out of it.'

'Supposing the girl has already talked?' said Levistien. 'These people 'ull know who's got her, and if they go to the police . . . '

'We've got to risk it,' snapped Syd. 'It's

a question of the devil and the deep blue sea. We can't leave her where she is. That definitely means trouble. The other way may mean trouble, but it may save the situation. We've got to take a chance.'

'Where are we going to take her?' asked Levistien dubiously.

'To 'The Flaming Dawn',' said Syd. 'It's up to Anitra and Pellissi then to see that she causes no more trouble.'

Levistien didn't like it at all, and said so plainly.

'I don't like it, either,' said Syd. 'But it's got to be done. Now we'll get Tim and Mark an' . . . '

'Sh-s-s,' whispered Levistien, suddenly stopping him. 'Somebody's coming out of the cottage!'

They had paused for their talk about opposite the white gate, and now, as they stepped back into the shadow of the tree, they saw the door open, and for a brief instant caught a glimpse of the figure that appeared on the threshold.

'The girl!' muttered Syd under his breath.

They heard the low murmur of voices,

and then the door shut and a slim form came quickly down the path.

'She's coming out,' whispered Levistien.

'Handed to us on a plate,' answered Syd. 'This is going to make things easy.'

The girl reached the gate, paused for a moment, and then began to walk briskly in the direction of Staines.

'Come on,' said Syd, 'after her. It's going to be as easy as falling off a log.'

With Levistien at his heels he hurried after the dim figure that was rapidly fading in the darkness.

'Take off your jacket,' muttered Syd. 'I'll grab her arms and you throw your jacket over her head.'

Levistien did as he was bidden. They were within a few yards of the girl when she heard them and looked round.

'Now!' said Syd, and rushed forward.

She started to run, but it was too late. Syd caught her by the arms from behind and Levistien flung his coat over her head and drew it tight. Her cry was muffled in the folds of cloth, but she struggled desperately, kicking wildly.

'Get her to the car,' panted Syd. 'Quick!'

Half carrying and half dragging, they got the struggling girl up the road to the waiting car.

'Mark, give us a hand,' called Syd as they reached it, and a big man got out and came to their assistance. They bundled the still struggling captive into the car, and the three of them got in beside her.

'Now drive like hell to 'The Flaming Dawn',' ordered Syd, and the car moved forward.

20

Mr. Buncle, thoroughly surprised and bewildered, gazed down at the limp form of the girl who had collapsed into his arms. But in spite of his astonishment he retained sufficient presence of mind to kick shut the front door. Whatever this strange woman was seeking help from was outside in the darkness of the night, and it was just as well to put a barrier between her and whatever it was as quickly as possible.

Having done that he called for assistance, and Carol and Colgate-Jones came hurriedly out of the sitting room.

'Good heavens, who's that?' demanded the clergyman as he saw Mr. Buncle's helpless burden. 'What's happened?'

'I don't know,' said Mr. Buncle. 'This woman was on the step when I opened the door, and . . . '

237

'It's Janice Gould!' broke in Carol, pushing past her uncle and staring at the white face lying in the crook of Mr. Buncle's arm. 'Is she hurt?'

Mr. Buncle shook his large head.

'No, she's only fainted, I think,' he replied. 'Would you help me carry her into the sitting room?'

'Certainly.' Colgate-Jones, to whom he had put the request, hastened forward. Between them they carried the unconscious Janice into the sitting room and laid her gently on the settee.

'I will get some restoratives,' said Mr. Buncle, and hurried away.

'How on earth did she get here?' said Carol, wrinkling her nose.

Colgate-Jones shook his head in perplexity.

'I've no idea,' he declared. 'But I must say I'm very pleased and relieved to see her. I never expected to,' he added.

'She ought to be able to tell us something when she comes round,' said Carol hopefully.

It was not long before she did come round. Mr. Buncle administered his 'restoratives', and in a few minutes Janice was sitting up blinking dazedly. She caught sight of Carol and Colgate-Jones and her eyes opened wide with astonishment.

'How — how did you get here?' she asked weakly.

'How did *you* get here?' replied Carol.

Janice pushed back her hair.

'I ran away from Anitra's house,' she said simply.

'Anitra!' exclaimed Carol. 'What has she . . . '

'I think,' broke in Mr. Buncle gently, 'that the young lady had better have a little nourishment before answering questions — if you will forgive my suggesting it.'

'It's a very excellent idea, Buncle,' said Colgate-Jones approvingly. 'You always hit on the right idea at the right moment.'

Mr. Buncle gave a deprecating and gratified cough.

'I will go and prepare some strong tea and a scrambled egg on toast,' he said, and once more took a hasty departure.

'Who is he?' asked Janice as the door

closed behind the little man.

Carol explained.

'It's a most amazing piece of luck my coming here,' exclaimed Janice. 'It was the first house I saw when that man was chasing me, and I just took a chance that somebody would be up.'

'We never expected to see you again, Miss Gould,' said Colgate-Jones gravely. 'We were convinced that you, like ourselves, had fallen foul of this Nazi group.'

'I think I did,' said Janice, settling herself more comfortably in a corner of the settee. 'I'm sure that woman Anitra and Pellissi are part of them. If they weren't they wouldn't have behaved as they did to me.'

'Look here!' burst out Carol, 'I'm dying to know exactly what they *did* do to you.'

Janice smiled.

'I'm sorry,' she said, 'I suppose I'm being very tantalizing. I'll tell you the whole story.'

She did so, and they listened in silence until she had finished.

'So you don't know what happened to

the letter that Mr. Clavering gave you?' said Carol, and Janice shook her head.

'If my coat is still at 'The Flaming Dawn',' she said, 'the letter is probably still in the lining.'

Mr. Buncle came in with a tray as Carol shot a quick glance at Colgate-Jones.

'We ought to tell Mr. Dene about that at once,' she said excitedly, and the clergyman nodded.

'Yes,' he said seriously. 'There is a chance that the coat is still there.'

'Don't you think that Anitra or Pellissi would have removed it?' said Janice, sipping gratefully at the tea which Mr. Buncle set before her. 'They would guess it was mine, wouldn't they?'

'They might,' said Carol. 'But they wouldn't know about the letter, would they? On the other hand, Anitra didn't remove it — she hadn't time — and Pellissi knew nothing about you until he came to the bungalow. Unless one of them went back after they had locked you in that room, I don't see when they could have removed it.'

She saw Mr. Buncle's large brown eyes looking from one to the other inquisitively and laughed.

'You don't know what we are talking about, do you?' she said. 'I think we had better tell you.'

She proceeded to do so with interjections from Colgate-Jones and Janice.

'It seems,' said Mr. Buncle, gently rubbing his large forehead when she had finished — 'it seems that there is little doubt that these people — er — the woman called Anitra and the man Pellissi, are engaged in something unlawful. It was obviously their guilty consciences that made them act towards you in the way they did — particularly the woman's.'

'They're definitely members of X.1's group,' declared Carol with conviction. 'I should think that 'The Flaming Dawn' was their headquarters . . . ' She stopped as she saw that Mr. Buncle was slowly shaking his head. 'You don't think so?' she demanded.

'I wouldn't presume to say that you are wrong, Miss Wray,' said Mr. Buncle diffidently. 'But it seems to me that this business regarding Miss — er — Gould has been handled too, shall I say, amateurishly to have emanated from this group controlled by X.1 . . . '

'But that was Anitra's fault,' interrupted Janice, with her mouth full of scrambled egg and toast. 'Pellissi was furious that she had done it, but of course he had to back her up.'

'I doubt,' said Mr. Buncle, still very apologetically, 'if X.1 would have in his employ a woman who was likely to behave impetuously, or a man either. The people who work for him are, I am sure, chosen with the greatest care. The whole success of his organization would depend on that.'

'There's a lot in what you say, Buncle,' put in Colgate-Jones, 'and, after all, you should know. You've been in this espionage business yourself. But these people, Anitra and Pellissi and the other man, must be afraid of something. Their actions are proof of that.'

'Oh, yes,' said Mr. Buncle, 'I wouldn't dream of disputing that. In fact I am only giving you my opinion. I may, of course, be entirely wrong.'

'Well, anyway,' said Carol, 'whether you are right or wrong I think Mr. Dene should be told about the coat and the letter. It's most important. It may save everything.'

'Yes, my dear, you're right,' said Colgate-Jones. 'I will go down to 'The Flaming Dawn' at once and tell him . . . '

'Oh, no, you won't,' said Carol quickly. 'I'll go . . . '

'Indeed you will do no such thing,' declared the vicar emphatically. 'It would be a highly dangerous proceeding . . . '

'Listen, Kupie,' said his niece, 'I'm sorry to spoil your fun. Oh, I know you're just dying to poke your nose into things, but this time you're going to do as you're told.'

'Really,' remonstrated Colgate-Jones.

'Really, nothing,' continued Carol. 'I'm going, and that is an end of the argument. If this coat of Janice's is still in the cloakroom, neither Mr. Dene nor Mr. Stacey will be able to do anything about it. But I can pretend that it's mine.'

'I think if anyone goes it should be me,' put in Janice.

'Nonsense,' said Carol, shaking her head. 'You're tired out and you need a good rest. No, it's no good arguing. I've made up my mind to go, and I'm going.' Her face set obstinately.

'You can't go to 'The Flaming Dawn' like that,' objected Colgate-Jones, eyeing her sketchy attire, which consisted of one of Mr. Buncle's bathrobes over her own tattered frock.

'Janice can lend me her clothes,' said Carol firmly. 'We're about the same size. So that's that!'

'But there's one other thing, and that's not so easily got over,' said the clergyman. 'How are you going to get there? Dene has taken the car, and there will be no trains or buses running at this hour.'

Carol looked at him in dismay.

'I hadn't thought of that,' she admitted. 'That's rather torn it, hasn't it?'

'I think I could arrange a means of transport,' remarked Mr. Buncle. 'I have a friend who possesses a small car. He lives at the end of the road in a small house with a red gate and red doors and window-sashes — you can't mistake it. In the circumstances I am sure he would take you, provided he could be assured that there would be no trouble over his using the petrol for such a purpose. I am sure Mr. Dene would see to that. I will ring him up and have a word with him, if you will excuse me.'

'Lovely!' exclaimed Carol. 'There you are! Come upstairs, Janice, and I'll change into your things.'

'I still think it would be better if I went — ' began Colgate-Jones, his jovial face marred by a troubled frown.

'Nonsense, Kupie,' said his niece. 'Now don't start an argument all over again. Come along, Janice.'

The two girls disappeared upstairs and Mr. Buncle went to the telephone to call up his friend. The Rev. Colgate-Jones stared uncertainly at his fingernails. He disliked the idea of Carol going, but he had to admit that she would probably be of more use to Dene than he would. Perhaps he ought to go with her, but there again he was uncertain. Dene had been very emphatic that he should remain with Buncle and keep in the background. If he appeared at 'The Flaming Dawn' he might upset whatever plans Dene had in mind. Reluctantly he came to the conclusion that he had better let Carol have her own way and see the thing through on her own.

Mr. Buncle was a long time at the telephone, and when he eventually came back he explained that he had some difficulty in getting a reply. His friend had been in bed. He was, however, provided Mr. Buncle would indemnify him against all trouble with the authorities, prepared to take Carol to 'The Flaming Dawn'.

'I have assured him that there will be no trouble over the petrol,' said Mr. Buncle. 'And he will have the car ready if Miss Wray will pick it up at his house. I suggested that he should call here, but his house is on the way, and he seemed to prefer that she should go there. It is only a little way away.'

Carol came down a few seconds later dressed in Janice's clothes, and looking as though they had been made for her.

'The house is at the end of the road on the left, and has red window-frames and doors,' she said. 'All right, I'll find it. Wish me luck, because if that letter is still there it may mean that all our troubles will be over.'

She left Mr. Buncle's cottage full of optimism, to walk straight into the arms of Syd and Levistien.

21

Michael Dene looked round the crowded dance-floor of 'The Flaming Dawn', but there was no sign of Stacey anywhere. He sat down at the table, poured himself out a drink, and tried to puzzle out what could have happened. The fair-haired girl had rejoined her two elderly companions and they were all three laughing and talking once more, but there was no sign of the dark man who had flicked him the warning. The man in grey, to whom he had referred, was dancing with his A.T.S. companion and appeared to be thoroughly enjoying himself. Dene got a close look at him as he passed near the table. The girl was laughing at something he was saying, and he never even glanced in Dene's direction. Was the message genuine, or had it been given in order to divert his attention away from the real people

249

who were dangerous — like a conjurer's patter designed to cover up a trick of sleight of hand? It was rather a feeble effort if that were the case, thought Dene. On the other hand, if it was genuine, who was the dark man and his three companions? Whoever he was, he obviously knew something. But he had vanished as effectively as Stacey.

Where was Stacey, and what had made him suddenly disappear in the short space of time that Dene had been gone? Perhaps that had been the reason for the message — to get him away from Stacey so that some plan concerning him could be put into action. But what plan, and how could the people concerned have foreseen that he would leave the dance-floor to read the message?

Dene lit a cigarette and idly watched the dancers while his mind tried to find a solution to these various problems. The fair girl was now dancing with one of the middle-aged men, while the other remained at their table smoking a cigar and sipping his whisky. The man in grey and the A.T.S. girl had gone back to their table, and he was mopping his face while she powdered her nose. Neither seemed to have any interest in anything other than themselves. There were more Service men here tonight than there had been on the Saturday — quite a number of R.A.F. men and a considerable sprinkling of Americans.

On the surface 'The Flaming Dawn' was just an ordinary road-house catering for the pleasure and amusement of those war-weary people who had the leisure, and the money, to enjoy its amenities. Only one or two of the better informed, thought Dene, knew of the sinister undercurrents that were cloaked by all the laughter and the noise and the music.

It seemed impossible that danger could lurk in such an atmosphere — that somewhere unknown and unsuspected the emissaries of the Third Reich schemed and plotted amid all this tawdry splendour — and yet Dene had had proof that such was the case. One of the people present among that motley crowd of pleasure-seekers might even be X.1 himself.

And Stacey had not returned.

Sitting at his table, outwardly calm and a little bored, but watchful and vigilant, Dene began to feel a twinge of uneasiness. What could have happened? Had something happened to arouse Stacey's suspicions — something so urgent that he had had to act at once, or had disaster overtaken him?

It was difficult to imagine how anything very serious could have happened to him in the midst of all these people. On that other occasion what had been done had been done under cover of darkness, but tonight there had been no failure of the lights, and in the brilliant glow from the myriad of rising suns surely it would have been impossible for even X.1 to spirit a man away against his will?

Stacey, therefore, must have gone of his own accord, and in that case it was certain that he had had a particularly good reason. It must, too, have been an urgent reason, or he would have waited for Dene's return. It seemed likely, therefore, that Stacey was 'on' to something. Dene sincerely hoped that he was. It would at least show that they had not wasted the evening, which was what he felt as though he were doing at the moment. Only five more days left! He felt a little coldness creep up his spine as he thought of it. Five more days to unearth the whole thing and stop X.1's scheme being carried out. And practically nothing to go on. The almost incoherent words of a dying man — a glimpse here and a glimpse there of something black and ugly staring — and that was all. It was a delicate situation. A false move might set the thin ice on which he walked cracking in all directions and send him and the country he loved plunging into the black depths beneath.

Dene felt the terrible responsibility weigh on him like a tangible burden. He knew the significance of the date June 21st. It was perfect timing. His thoughts were disturbed by the sudden appearance of Pellissi. He came out from the curtained archway at the side of the band dais and surveyed the dance-floor. His face was pale and he wore a worried frown. He seemed to be looking for someone, for his little eyes darted hither and thither in all directions. After a minute or two he turned and went back through the archway without having, apparently, found whom he sought. Or perhaps he was just taking a casual survey of his establishment.

Was Pellissi important? That was the difficulty with this business — to know who the people were who were important and who were not. The man in grey — the dark man who had given the warning — the fair girl and the two elderly men at the table — were they all members of the Nazi group, and if not just who was? That the place itself was important Dene hadn't a doubt. It was here that Clavering had spent most of his time, and it was from here that Dene and the others had been spirited away to the house at Sythe and their interview with X.1. It was here that Janice Gould had walked across the dance-floor to the cloakroom and never come back. The place was important enough, but who were the important people in it?

Michael Dene smoked and pondered,

waiting for something that would give him a lead — a slight sign, an overheard word, but it grew late and nothing happened.

By degrees the crowd sitting at the tables or dancing began to thin. By two's and three's they drifted away until at last only a scattered few remained. Dene, glancing at his watch, saw that it was nearly one o'clock. The place would be closing soon. The man in grey and the A.T.S. girl were already preparing to leave. The two elderly business men and the fair girl — all three a little drunk — were crossing the floor to the exit.

Dene decided that he might as well make a move, too. He had shown himself, and the Nazi group must be well aware by this time that he was still in the land of the living. It was clear that they had no intention of starting anything at 'The Flaming Dawn', at any rate not inside. Whatever move was contemplated was more likely due to be put into practice when he left. Or perhaps their policy was to follow him in order to find out where the others were. It was no use waiting. He had had very little sleep on the previous night, and was feeling thoroughly tired and weary.

There was still nearly half of Stacey's bottle of Johnnie Walker left, and he beckoned to a yawning waiter to remove it for a future occasion. The man had just started to walk towards him when from somewhere in the back of the building came a shrill scream. It was followed almost instantly by two shots fired in rapid succession. The few remaining people at the tables started to their feet, those who had reached the exit stopped and turned in startled surprise. Through the curtained archway at the side of the band dais staggered Pellissi, his white shirt-front splashed with blood. For a moment he stood swaying, clawing at the air, and then he collapsed in a twitching heap on the polished dance-floor.

★ ★ ★

When Michael Dene left him to read the message which the dark man had so adroitly flicked on to their table in passing, Frank Stacey's one thought was curiosity to know what it contained. He guessed that Dene would not take long to find out and return, and so he awaited his coming with as much patience as he could muster. And then as two men passed quickly by his table he heard something which drove all thought of the dark man and the message from his mind. It was only a single word, but it was sufficient to bring him to immediate alertness. It was the one word '*tooth-paste*'. What went before or what followed was just a vague murmur, but that one word stood out as though it had been shouted through a megaphone. Out of the tail of his eye he managed to catch a glimpse of the man who had uttered it. He was a nondescript-looking individual of medium height, and his companion was short and stout. They had come in about twenty minutes before, and had a drink at one of the tables on the far side of the room. Neither Dene nor Stacey had taken very much notice of them. Now, apparently, they had decided to leave, for they were walking quickly towards the exit.

Stacey hesitated for the fraction of a second and then made up his mind to follow them.

Of course it might be nothing more than a coincidence. 'Toothpaste' was not an uncommon word, and could quite easily have been part of a purely ordinary and innocent conversation. But if it was a coincidence, it was a very queer one, and Stacey decided that he wasn't taking any chances. Here, thrown at him by the hand of a beneficent Providence, was a faint clue that, followed up, might lead to the solution of the whole riddle. He got up as casually as possible and sauntered after the two men. They passed through the exit doors and collected their hats and coats from the attendant in charge. They put them on in a leisurely, unhurried manner, chatting all the while, lit cigarettes, and finally strolled out.

Stacey grabbed his hat and coat quickly, flung the man who gave them to him a tip, and followed. 'The Flaming Dawn' had, prior to its conversion into a road-house, been a garage, complete with the usual array of petrol pumps in a semi-circular bay in front of the entrance. The petrol pumps had been removed and this bay now formed a more or less imposing approach to the place, lined with shrubs in pots and used, on occasions, as an auxiliary car park to the large one in the rear of the building. In these days there were very few cars and none in this entrance crescent, so that Stacey, when he came out on to the top of the shallow steps, had a clear view of his quarry, or as clear as the darkness of the night allowed. They were walking slowly, side by side, down the left-hand driveway, and as they turned through the pillared opening into the roadway Stacey went after them. Except for the two men he was following, the road was deserted, and he realized that he would have to be very careful if he was to avoid their becoming aware that he was tracking them. He dropped as far behind as he dared without risk of losing sight of them altogether and strolled along in their wake.

Next to 'The Flaming Dawn' was a

short arcade of shops and then the road became lined with large houses that stood well back in imposing gardens full of trees and shrubbery. At one time these houses had been private residences and some of them were still, but for the most part they had degenerated into boarding-houses, private hotels, and offices. A considerable number of them had been requisitioned by the Government for soldiers, and some of the gardens were full of lorries and jeeps. Farther along there were two houses that had suffered severe bomb damage. Their broken windows had been boarded up and the gaping roofs covered with tarpaulin. The two men had passed these and Stacey was just in the act of doing so when from the dark opening of the second house, where once the gate had hung, a man stepped out suddenly and unexpectedly. Before Stacey quite realized what was happening the man was at his side and the unmistakable muzzle of a pistol was rammed hard into his ribs.

'If you make a sound or attempt to run, you're as good as dead,' grunted the newcomer. 'If you're sensible you'll do exactly as you're told and save a lot of trouble.'

With the pistol grinding into his side, Stacey decided to be sensible.

'What do you want?' he asked, though the question was unnecessary.

'What I've got — you!' was the answer. 'Don't stop — keep walking.'

The two men in front had stopped and were waiting. In a short while Stacey and the other man joined them.

'Well, well, so it worked,' greeted the taller of the two, addressing Stacey. 'You fell for our little trap very nicely.'

'So what?' demanded Stacey.

'That you will see in due course,' was the answer. 'Do you know what a hostage is? I am sure you do. Well, *you* are a hostage and you will be the means of rendering Michael Dene and the rest of you harmless to the Third Reich.'

22

Monday — 1 a.m.

Carol, as she sat between the two men in the speeding car, realized in a flash of intuition what had happened. They had mistaken her for Janice! In spite of her danger and the physical discomfort of the jacket which enveloped her head and made breathing difficult, she couldn't help smiling as she thought of the effect her unexpected appearance would have on Pellissi and Anitra. They were expecting one girl and they would get another. A blonde instead of a brunette. The shock they would receive would be worth witnessing. The mistake had been a very plausible one, for she was wearing Janice's clothes, and the scarf round her hair had concealed her colouring.

After her first attempt to break away she had ceased to struggle, realizing that it was merely a useless waste of energy.

'Well, that's that!' remarked Syd. 'As easy as kiss your hand.'

Levistien grunted.

'It saved us a lot of trouble — her coming out when she did,' went on Syd. 'I wonder where she was makin' for?'

'Why don't you ask her?' said Levistien. He was still feeling uneasy about the whole business. This was not in his line at all, and once again he heartily wished that he had never had anything to do with it. A certain amount of easy money was one thing, but this was a coat of another colour.

'I'm not going to ask her because she couldn't answer with that coat over her head,' said Syd, 'an' I've no intention of taking it off.'

Carol, who could just hear the conversation, wondered what they would say if they knew where she had been going, and why. Curiously enough she felt no fear, her only feeling in the matter was one of intense curiosity to see the outcome of the matter. She might have been a little less unperturbed could she have foreseen what the night held in store, but she was mercifully ignorant of this. The men beside her did not talk any more as the car sped onwards, but she heard the scratch of a match as the one on her left lit a cigarette.

Presently the car slowed down and turned, and she guessed that they had reached 'The Flaming Dawn'. She was right, for the car came to a stop and the men beside her shifted. She was grasped by the arms and helped out, and a voice close to her head said:

'Don't you make a sound or it 'ull be the worse for you.'

The warning was unnecessary, for she had no intention of either making a sound or struggling. Both, she knew, would be useless.

She was led from the car over a strip of ground, up three steps, and then through a door and into a building. She could feel carpet under her feet. It was the way Anitra had taken Janice on the previous night, but she did not know that.

'Here you are,' said the man on her left, and a woman's voice exclaimed:

'So you've got her.'

'Yes, we've got her,' retorted the man. 'It's up to you an' Pellissi to keep her.'

'Don't worry about that,' said the woman, and Carol concluded rightly that it was Anitra who spoke. 'Take that coat off her.'

Now for the big sensation, thought Carol, as the coat was whisked from her head. A flood of light made her blink, and she saw that she was in an office. Behind a large desk sat the fat figure of Pellissi, frowning and biting his nails. Behind him stood the green-clad figure of Anitra.

'Good evening,' said Carol coolly.

Pellissi's podgy hand dropped from his thick lips and his mouth gaped open. His utter astonishment made him look stupid. Anitra's reaction was not so marked.

She gave a slight start and her eyes opened very wide and then narrowed.

'Who's this?' She almost snarled the words.

'What do you mean?' exclaimed Syd. 'This is the girl . . . '

'It's not the girl, you fool!' snapped Anitra. 'You've made a mistake . . . '

'She's wearing the same clothes and

she came out of the cottage,' began Levistien, and was interrupted by a wail from the stout Pellissi.

'Oh, my God — this is terrible,' he groaned. 'What have you done now . . . ?'

'Shut up!' said Anitra. 'This is not the girl, but she's one of the people who were with her last night . . . '

'What does that matter?' cried Pellissi, beating on the desk with his fist. 'What does it matter who she is? You've ruined us with your meddling . . . '

'I told you to shut up!' Anitra turned on him like an angry tigress, and Pellissi cowered back before the blazing expression in her eyes as though he expected physical violence.

'When you've quite finished arguing among yourselves,' remarked Carol, 'perhaps you'll kindly explain the meaning of this tomfoolery.'

'It's anything but tomfoolery.' Anitra was still in such a rage that her voice shook. 'You'll find that out. Your friend wouldn't talk, but perhaps you'll be more sensible.'

'Certainly,' said Carol calmly. 'What

shall we talk about? The war, the weather . . . '

'We'll talk about *you*,' said Anitra, 'and you'll do the talking! What's your object in spying about this place?'

'Spying?' said Carol. She shrugged her shoulders and looked at the two men who stood near her. 'What does she mean?' she asked innocently.

'You know very well what I mean,' said Anitra. She had recovered her self-control and her voice was steady and cold. Carol thought as she looked at her that she was infinitely more dangerous in this mood.

'I just don't know what you're talking about,' she said. 'I think you must be mad. You kidnap my friend because she goes to the cloakroom, and now you've kidnapped me and accuse me of spying. You're crazy.'

'Am I?' Anitra took two steps forward, lifted her slender hand and struck Carol across the mouth. 'Now don't play about with me. I'm in no mood for it.'

The blow had been swift and unexpected. It cut Carol's lip and left a red mark across the lower part of her suddenly white face.

'Now I know you're mad,' she said, and the contempt in her voice was like the lash of a whip. It flicked Anitra on the raw and she snatched up a heavy ruler from the desk and raised it over the girl's head.

'Stop her — for God's sake stop her!' cried Pellissi, starting up from his chair. 'She will ruin us with her stupidity and her temper . . . '

Syd shot out a hand and caught Anitra's wrist before the blow could fall.

'Don't be a fool,' he snapped. 'You're going a bit too far. Pellissi's right. You've got us all in a tight jamb, and the way you're going on is going to get us in a worse one. Curb that damned temper of yours and behave sensibly.'

'Let me go — you scum!' hissed Anitra, and plain, naked murder glared from her eyes. 'Let me go.'

'I'm not letting you go,' said Syd. He gave a vicious twist to her wrist and the ruler fell with a clatter to the floor. 'I believe the girl's right and you are crazy.'

'Anitra, Syd, Levistien.' Pellissi waved his hands frantically in the air for attention. 'Let us try and be sensible. Let us try and undo this mischief. My dear miss,' he turned to Carol. 'Please to allow me to apologize for this lady's badness, and for any inconvenience that you have suffered. It is all a mistake, and I am very sorry that such a thing should have happened to you. But Anitra — it is she who is to blame, she is so impulsive. She thinks your friend was spying, and it angered her. In running these places one has occasionally to go outside the law, you understand? It is difficult, without offending, to refuse people a little drink, you understand? It is really nothing, but the laws are very hard on such things. Anitra is part owner of 'The Flaming Dawn' with me, and she does not like to see anything happen that would result in the place being closed. It is understandable, and there are always people trying to make trouble with the police. Anitra thought that your friend was one. It was a mistake and she acted foolishly. I told her she was foolish, but she would not listen. Your friend was treated well. She shall be recompensed — a nice present — anything that she would choose. And you, too, my dear young lady. Let us not take this little mistake seriously, let us treat it as a good joke. You understand it is really only Anitra's impulsive nature. Her temper is bad, but she is a good girl . . . '

'Oh, cut the sob stuff!' broke in Anitra impatiently. 'You're not getting anywhere. She doesn't believe a word you're saying, and I don't blame her. It wouldn't take in a child of ten.'

Pellissi made a gesture of despair, and Carol felt quite sorry for him. He had tried so hard, even if, as Anitra had said, his effort had been a little childish.

'It's no good trying the soft soap,' went on Anitra. 'I'll admit we're in a tight corner, but are only to get out of it in a drastic way. I don't care what you say, both these women are spies in the employ of the authorities and the only way we can be safe is to ensure that they are not in a position to talk.'

She looked significantly from one to

the other, and it was Levistien who spoke first.

'I'll have no hand in it,' he exclaimed emphatically, and shook his head.

'Nor I,' said Syd.

'You'd rather go to prison, I suppose?' sneered Anitra.

'I'd rather go to prison than swing, and what you're advocating, in plain words, is — murder.'

'No, no,' Pellissi spread his hands. 'Anitra would not suggest such a thing . . . '

'I wish you'd be quiet,' said Anitra viciously. 'Look here, all of you . . . '

What she was going to say was interrupted by a sudden knock on the door.

Instantly there was complete silence.

'Who's that?' whispered Syd.

Anitra shook her head.

'I don't know. I'll see. Take the girl over in that alcove.' She nodded to a curtained recess in one corner.

Syd grasped Carol's arm and dragged her over as Anitra went and unlocked the door.

271

'What — ' she began, and broke off as a man pushed his way into the office.

'I'm Detective Inspector Corpen of the Special Branch, New Scotland Yard,' said the dark man who had given Dene the warning message earlier in the evening. 'I want you, Pellissi.'

'Me — you want me?' Pellissi faced him, his flabby cheeks the colour of lard.

'Yes, you,' said Corpen curtly. 'And you, too,' he added, looking at Anitra.

'What for?' she demanded.

'I'm taking you into custody on a charge of illicitly acquiring goods contrary to the Defence of the Realm Act,' said Corpen. 'I have to warn you that anything you say may be used in evidence . . . '

'But this is nonsense,' cried Pellissi. 'I know nothing of such things . . . '

'You wouldn't,' snapped Corpen. 'I've never arrested a man yet who did know anything about the offence he was charged with. However, you can argue it out with the magistrate. Get your things on and come with me.'

'This is an outrage,' said Pellissi. 'You

are accusing me of black market dealings?'

'Yes,' Corpen nodded. 'I'm accusing you and this woman here of just that. And it's no good you trying to bluff because I've got all the proof in the world.'

'I'm afraid you've made a very great mistake, Inspector,' said Anitra smoothly.

'You needn't be afraid, because I haven't made any mistake,' retorted Corpen. 'I and my sergeant here' — he turned to a quiet, thickset man who had slipped unobtrusively into the office while he had been speaking — 'have had this place under observation for the past six months. We know all about the stuff that has been coming in and going out at all hours of the night . . . '

'That was legitimate stock used for running this place,' said Anitra quickly. 'You can't . . . '

'Are you acquainted with a man called Rignold?' asked Corpen, and Anitra's expression changed. 'You sold him fifty cases of tea last week, stipulating that the money for it was to be paid in one pound notes. Rignold bought that tea acting on my instructions — he is, in fact, one of my men. You tried to sell him at the same time a consignment of cigars, which had been smuggled from Ireland . . . '

'I know nothing about what you say,' cried Pellissi. 'If such things have been done from here it was without my knowledge . . . '

'It's no good, Pellissi,' said Corpen, shaking his head. 'You know all about it. You've been in the black market for nearly eighteen months, and now you've been caught. Nothing you can say or do is going to get you out of it.'

'It was not me,' declared Pellissi. 'It was not my idea at all. I was talked into it by Anitra. It was she who organized the whole scheme . . . '

'Shut up, you snivelling little squeaker!' snapped Anitra, but the terrified Pellissi was not to be silenced.

'I could not help myself,' he protested. 'You understand the position, Mr Corpen? What could I do . . . '

'You were as much in it as anybody,' broke in Syd. 'You took your share, didn't you?'

'I was completely under the thumb of these people,' said Pellissi. 'I had no say of my own. I was forced to do what they wanted. I did what I did under — how do you put it? — duress, that is it. It should be taken into consideration . . .'

'Everything will be taken into consideration,' said Corpen, eyeing the perspiring Pellissi with open disgust. 'You'd better reserve all your explanations until you get into court. I can't waste any more time . . .'

But Pellissi hadn't finished.

'I could tell you something that the Government would like to know,' he said. 'That would go in my favour, wouldn't it? If I could give you some useful information . . .'

He stopped suddenly and his face went a ghastly greenish white. With eyes that were nearly popping out of his head he was staring at the door through which Levistien and Syd had brought Carol earlier.

Corpen swung round, and as he did so Pellissi screamed. In the doorway, which was partly open, stood a man, and even as

Corpen caught sight of him, he raised his hand. There were two bright flashes, followed by two thunderous reports. Pellissi staggered, and his shirt front suddenly grew red. He gave a choking grunt and then, half running and half stumbling, he fled through the open office door that led to the dance-floor of 'The Flaming Dawn'.

'Look after him,' said Corpen to the sergeant, and darted to the outer door just as the shooter pulled it shut in his face.

23

Michael Dene was the first to reach the inert figure of Pellissi, and one glance at the staring, glazing eyes told him that the man was dead. The remaining habitués of 'The Flaming Dawn', recovering from their momentary astonished stupor, crowded round, and a flood of questions bombarded Dene from all sides.

Through this chattering crowd a thick-set man forced his way to Dene's side and dropped on one knee beside Pellissi.

'He's quite dead,' said Dene, 'but a doctor should be sent for at once, all the same.'

'Yes, sir,' agreed the sergeant. He got up, and his searching eyes quickly picked out the head waiter, and he beckoned to the man.

'Telephone for the nearest doctor,' he

ordered curtly when the man came. 'Now, all of you, keep back there,' he went on, addressing the people around. 'The best thing you can all do is to leave. This place is in the hands of the police, and will be closed until further notice.'

As the curious crowd began to drift reluctantly away, Dene edged closer to the sergeant.

'You are a police officer?' he inquired, and it was a statement rather than a question. 'Take a look at this.'

He held out his hand under the man's nose. In the palm was a green card enclosed in a little leather case with a cellophane front. The sergeant took one glance at it, and his face changed.

'All right, sir,' he said respectfully. 'I didn't know you were in on this business. I'm Sergeant Bratt.'

'How did it happen?' asked Dene, and Bratt told him.

'H'm, black market, eh?' said Dene. 'Well, I'm not surprised to hear it. However, that's your side of it. I'm after bigger game than black marketeers.'

'Oh,' said the sergeant, 'I thought you

were on this business . . . '

'I thought I was until you explained,' replied Dene. 'But my interest is no longer in Pellissi, but in the man who shot him. You say he said he was in a position to divulge information that would be of interest to the Government?'

'Yes, sir,' said Bratt.

'And then this man appeared suddenly at the door and shot him?'

'That's right, sir.'

'I'd like to get that man . . . ' began Dene, and was interrupted by a voice behind him.

'So would I, Mr. Dene.'

He turned and found the dark man behind him. With him were Anitra, Syd and Levistien.

'Look after those three, will you, Bratt?' said Corpen. 'I recognized you earlier this evening, Mr. Dene,' he went on. 'We've never met, but you were pointed out to me a few months ago by a fellow at the F.O., and I never forget a face.'

He introduced himself and Dene shook hands.

'Glad to meet you, Inspector,' he said.

'Thanks for that warning.'

'Thought it might be useful,' said Corpen. 'I happened to hear that fat fellow in grey talking about you to his girl friend. He seemed to know all about you, and so I thought I'd tip you off.'

'To his girl friend — the A.T.S.?' said Dene. 'H'm, surprising in what unexpected places you find these people.'

'What people?' asked Corpen.

'Nazis,' answered Dene. 'I'm after a group of particularly dangerous Nazi agents, who've got a scheme that may be very damaging to this country if they are able to carry it out.'

Corpen pursed his lips and gave a silent whistle.

'So that's what this fellow Pellissi was talking about,' he said, 'and that's why he was shot.'

'The man who did it got away?' asked Dene, and Corpen nodded.

'Yes, worse luck,' he answered. 'I couldn't see a sign of him.'

'I've got three men outside,' said Dene. 'They may pick him up. They were there . . .'

He broke off and stared in genuine astonishment at the girl who, at that moment, appeared from the entrance to the ladies' cloakroom.

'Miss Wray!' he exclaimed. 'How on earth did you get here?'

'They brought me,' said Carol, and pointed to the discomfited Levistien and the sullen-faced Syd. 'They thought I was Janice Gould . . .'

She explained briefly what had happened at the cottage and her subsequent adventure.

'I've just been to see if Janice's coat was still in the cloakroom,' she said. 'When all the excitement started nobody seemed to care very much what I did, so I thought it was a good opportunity. The woman in charge says she knows nothing about it.'

'We'll have her in,' said Dene, and his eyes were sparkling with excitement. 'If we could only find that letter it might save a lot of time . . .'

'That's what I thought,' said Carol. 'That's why I suggested coming along to tell you about it.'

The cloakroom attendant was sent for

and closely questioned, but she strenu-
ously denied all knowledge of the coat.
When she had closed the cloakroom on
the previous night there was nothing left
behind. She seemed an honest enough
woman, and Dene believed her. Somehow
or other the people he was up against had
got hold of Janice's fur coat and
Clavering's letter.

Dene tried Anitra. If Pellissi had known
something it was more than possible that
this woman also knew. But all he could
get out of Anitra was a strenuous denial.
If Pellissi had done anything for, or got
mixed up with, any Nazi group, she had
known nothing about it. And this she
stuck to in spite of all Dene's efforts to
shake her.

With the death of Pellissi she had
changed. All the tigerishness had gone
out of her and she stood aloof, a slim
figure in emerald green, cold, distant, and
slightly contemptuous.

The doctor arrived, and was almost
immediately followed by the police,
whom Corpen had telephoned for.
Anitra, Levistien, and Syd were taken

away, and after the doctor's examination Pellissi was taken away too.

Michael Dene found himself with Corpen, Carol, and Sergeant Bratt in the empty and deserted 'Flaming Dawn'.

The lights still blazed from the rising suns, shining on empty tables and empty glasses and bottles, on a litter of empty cigarette cartons and crowded ashtrays. The place looked tawdry and tired, like an old woman who had painted herself up for an evening out and soon after it was over had removed her make-up.

It all looked a little cheap and nasty. The smoke-laden atmosphere, stale with fading perfume and the faint reek of spirits, was curiously depressing. At least Dene found it so. Maybe it was due to the fact that he had made no further progress in his task. There was not much point in his waiting any longer, and he went in search of Corpen to tell him that he was leaving. He found him in Pellissi's office going through a mass of papers and documents.

'There's enough evidence here to convict all of 'em over and over again,' said Corpen, yawning. 'It looks as if I shall be here most of the night. By the way, I shall want Miss Wray's address and the other young lady's. They'll be needed as witnesses.'

Dene gave him Mr. Buncle's address, said good night, and went to pick up Carol. They went in search of the car in which Dene and Stacey had driven to 'The Flaming Dawn' and found it occupying a position of solitary state in the car park. Dene took his place at the wheel, and Carol got in beside him and sank back with a sigh of relief. As Dene drove slowly out of the car park to the road he looked about for some sign of the three men who were supposed to be covering his movements, but there was no evidence of their existence.

He was more than a little puzzled over this. They were picked men — thoroughly reliable, and they should have been somewhere about, but they had disappeared as completely as Stacey. And what had happened to him?

As he ran out into the road and turned the radiator of the car in the direction of

Mr. Buncle's little cottage, his thoughts were busy on these two minor problems, the solution to both of which, had he but known it, was to reach him soon after his arrival at his destination.

24

Monday — 2.30 a.m.

When Dene and Carol reached Mr. Buncle's little cottage they found the eccentric owner, Colgate-Jones, and Janice Gould in a state of almost feverish anxiety. The reason for this, they discovered, was concerned entirely with Carol. About twenty minutes after she had left, Mr. Buncle's friend, who had agreed to drive her to 'The Flaming Dawn', had rung up to say he was ready and how long would she be. Mr. Buncle had informed him that she was already on her way and should be with him in a few minutes. At the expiration of a further quarter of an hour he had rung again to say that she had not arrived. Since it could not have taken her so long to walk the distance between the two houses they had instantly become alarmed. Mr. Buncle and Colgate-Jones had gone out to see if there was any sign of the missing girl. They had walked down to Mr. Buncle's friend's house and found him still waiting. Convinced by now that Carol had met with serious trouble on her way, and deciding that Anitra was probably at the bottom of it, they had gone to the house which Janice had described. The front door was open and the place, which they had searched, was completely deserted. There was nothing for it but to return to Mr. Buncle's cottage. Colgate-Jones had thought of getting Mr. Buncle's friend to drive him to 'The Flaming Dawn', but second thoughts had shown him that this might jeopardize Dene's plans and could do very little good. Anxiously they had discussed the situation and were still discussing it when Dene and Carol had arrived and put an end to their doubts and fears.

They listened interestedly while Dene and the girl discussed the evening's adventures in detail.

'And that is that,' finished Dene, wearily lighting a cigarette. 'It's been an exciting evening, but it's got us no further towards our main objective.'

'So that was why this woman Anitra

and Pellissi were so disturbed when she found Miss Gould was, as she thought, spying,' remarked Colgate-Jones. 'It had nothing to do with the X.1 business at all.'

Dene shook his head.

'Except that Pellissi knew something,' he replied. 'That's why he was killed.'

'Do you think Anitra was speaking the truth when she said she didn't know anything about it?' asked Janice.

'Yes,' answered Dene. 'I believe she was. It wasn't so much what she said as her expression that makes me think so. The dealings that Pellissi had with the Nazi group were, I am sure, a sideline of his own. If Anitra had known anything I believe she would have been shot, too.'

'Do you think the stout man in grey was one of the group?' inquired Colgate-Jones.

'Yes, I'm pretty sure of that,' said Dene, 'and his A.T.S. friend, too.'

'But surely if she was in the A.T.S. she couldn't be,' said Janice in astonishment.

'Why not?' Dene smiled wryly. 'There are 60,000 known Germans in this country, and quite a number who are not known as Germans and who are not, strictly speaking, of German origin, but are just pro-Nazi. They don't wear Swastikas in their hats and Iron Crosses on their watch-chains and say 'Heil Hitler'. If they did they would be no use to the Third Reich. They behave in an exemplary fashion and are very much for Britain and freedom and the downfall of the Nazi order. They are loyal to Germany — they will tell you that openly — but not Hitlerite Germany. They have no use for that. They will tell you tales of the suffering they have seen under Hitler's rule and tell you also that the majority of the German people are of the same opinion. That war was not the wish of the people but of the Nazi leaders, conveniently forgetting that it was the people of Germany who put Hitler and his gang in power, and that without the backing of the people there *could* have been no war. They will tell you all this and smile up their sleeves if you are gullible enough to believe it. They will tell you that when the war is over not to be too hard on Germany because it will be the people who will suffer, and every time a Bishop gets up and decries the bombing of Berlin they hug themselves because he's doing their work for them. I know Germany — and the Germans. Twice they have let loose the dogs of war upon the world — this second time owing to the muddled leadership of MacDonald, Baldwin and Chamberlain. Unless we pursue victory to its logical conclusion *this* time, disarm Germany and keep her disarmed, wipe her out once and for all as a Power, we shall only lay the foundation for a third war in twenty or thirty years' time.'

'Agreed,' said Colgate-Jones heartily. 'You speak bluntly, Dene, but you speak the truth.'

'I foresaw this war years ago,' said Michael Dene, a little bitterly, 'and I constantly warned the Government, but they would have none of me. Winston Churchill did the same and they would have none of him either. He was a warmonger, I was making mountains out of mole-hills. The Government then was like of lot of ostriches with their heads in the sand. And don't forget that a number of those men are *still* in power. It's them I'm afraid of when the time comes for dealing with Germany.' He got up abruptly. 'Here am I talking when I ought to be doing,' he said. 'There's X.1 and his crew to be dealt with.'

He began to pace restlessly up and down the room.

'Well,' remarked Colgate-Jones with a glance at the clock, 'I don't see what more can be done tonight. The best thing we can all do is to go to bed. We all need rest . . .'

'I'm worried about Stacey,' said Dene with a frown. 'I can't think what can have happened to him, or, for that matter, to Denham, Makeham, and Henway. They all appear to have vanished off the face of the earth, and I can't account for it.'

He sounded a little irritable, the result, as Colgate-Jones guessed, of anxiety and over-tiredness.

'I should think that the most likely explanation is that they've struck something,' said the clergyman. 'Listen, Dene, you've got to relax. It's not a bit of use wearing yourself out . . . '

And at that moment the telephone bell shrilled suddenly. Mr. Buncle was out of the room in an instant, and almost immediately, so it seemed, was back again.

'Mr. Stacey is on the telephone and wants to speak to you,' he said, and there was just a hint of excitement in his voice. 'He says that it is urgent.'

Dene hurried to the instrument and put the receiver to his ear.

'Dene this end,' he said, and immediately Frank Stacey's voice came over the wire.

'Can you come right away to Staines police-station?' he said. 'We've got three of X.1's bright boys here and I'd like you to see 'em.'

Dene wasted no time in asking questions over the phone.

'I'll come at once,' he said. 'Good work, Stacey.'

He hung up the receiver and went back to the sitting room. Briefly he explained, and Carol gave a little crow of delight.

'Can I come, too?' she asked, but Dene shook his head.

'I think I'd better go alone,' he said. 'The rest of you can take the advice Colgate-Jones gave me — go to bed.'

He was gone before the indignant girl could think of a suitable retort.

During the drive from Mr. Buncle's house to the police-station at Staines, Dene broke all the speed regulations that were ever made. The time he took to do the journey must have been a record to judge from the astonishment on Frank Stacey's face as he walked into the charge-room.

'Good Lord!' he greeted. 'How did you make it? Did you fly?'

'I drove a little fast,' said Dene. 'Now tell me all about it. Where are these three men?'

'Locked up in one of the cells,' said Stacey. 'Henway, Denham and Makeham are in the Superintendent's room . . . '

'How did you manage to get hold of these men?' interrupted Dene. 'What happened?'

Stacey gave a brief account of what had

occurred at 'The Flaming Dawn' after Dene had left him.

'I'll admit,' he said ruefully, 'that I fell into the trap very prettily. It was cleverly thought out, and I don't suppose I should be here now if it hadn't been for Henway, Makeham and Denham. With that fellow's gun in my ribs I hadn't got an earthly. But our men had seen me leave 'The Flaming Dawn' after those two Nazis, and guessed that I was following 'em. And they followed me. They intervened and put a stop to the little scheme to bring me as a bait to get you, though Henway got a nasty wound in his arm when the man with the pistol showed fight. He's had first-aid, but I think he ought to go and have it seen to. He wouldn't leave, however, until you had arrived.'

'We'll go and see them now,' said Dene, 'and then have a word with the prisoners.'

Stacey made a grimace as he led the way across the charge-room to a door on the opposite side.

'You'll be lucky if you get anything out of *them*,' he said. 'They've just remained stubbornly dumb ever since we got 'em.'

He opened the door and they went in to the small office.

A big man sat behind the desk in the little room, and grouped before him, smoking, were Henway, Makeham and Denham.

'Hello, chief,' greeted Makeham. 'This is Superintendent Dolittle, of the Staines police. We've got those birds locked up in one of the cells . . . '

'So I understand,' said Dene. 'You've done remarkably well all of you. I'm very glad to meet you, Superintendent.'

The uniformed man behind the desk stretched out a large hand and gripped Dene's.

'Pleased to meet you, too, sir,' he said. 'I understand these men we've got belong to a Nazi spy group?'

Dene nodded.

'A very dangerous group,' he said.

'Is that so, sir?' said the Superintendent stolidly. 'Well, that sort of thing is a bit out of my line, but, as I was telling these gentlemen, I'm willing to help in any way I can. You'd like to see them, I expect?'

'Yes,' said Dene, and refused the Superintendent's suggestion that they should be brought up. He sent Henway to find a doctor to have his wound properly attended to, and, accompanied by Stacey and Dolittle, went down to the cells.

The three men were sitting side by side on the pallet bed. They looked up as the cell door was opened, but their faces were expressionless. Dene, as he looked at them, thought he had seldom seen anyone who was less likely to arouse suspicion. They looked the typical type of English middle-class business man. They were middle-aged and neatly dressed, and had the appearance of being completely innocuous.

They had produced identity cards which looked genuine, but which Dene concluded were clever fakes, since the names on them were undeniably English. It was proved later that he was wrong. When inquiries were instituted it was found that the cards were genuine, and that the owners, although of German origin, had been established in England for so long under the names they bore that no one had ever dreamed of questioning their right to them.

For over two and a half hours he questioned them, but without result. They stubbornly refused to answer anything.

'In Germany they'd be *made* to talk,' said Stacey when Dene wearily gave it up and they returned to the Superintendent's office. 'The Gestapo would soon find a way of loosing their tongues.'

Dene agreed.

'This is not Germany, thank God,' he said, 'but sometimes I wish one could adopt some of her methods.'

He left instructions with the Superintendent regarding the prisoners and drove back with Stacey to Mr. Buncle's, Makeham, Henway and Denham following in a police car which Dolittle had lent them.

Dene was tired and dispirited.

The night had been a trying and heavy one, and had resulted in practically nothing. They had got three minor members of the group, who refused to talk, but they were no nearer to the really important objective — the finding of X.1 and the prevention of the signal which was to let loose a flood of destruction over the land.

25

Tuesday — 12 Noon

Michael Dene paced restlessly up and down the study at the vicarage, his hands clasped behind his back, his brows drawn together. His face was pale and thin, and there were marks under his eyes that testified to worry and lack of sleep. And, in truth, he had slept very little since his return from the police-station at Staines to Mr. Buncle's cottage in the early hours of Monday morning.

After barely three hours' rest he had got up, and before anyone else was stirring he was at the telephone. He had got on to Scotland Yard, secured the private address of the Commissioner, and disturbed that gentleman's rest in more senses than one. As a result, the police all over the country, including Scotland and Northern Ireland, had been warned to look out for anything suspicious that might put them on the track of the people who were being used by X.1 in the fulfilment of his scheme. All known agitators and strike leaders were to be watched, and any member of the number of queer sects which were known to exist. Dene had not been very hopeful that this would lead to any good results. It was a precaution and that was all. The plot had been too carefully planned, in his opinion, for any of the people concerned in its carrying out to be in a position to give it away; that was, of course, with the exception of the actual handful who were in control. Those who would carry it out would not, he concluded, receive their instructions until the last possible moment. They would know nothing and, knowing nothing, could give nothing away.

Again and again the three men in custody had been questioned, but they maintained their policy of silence.

'The Flaming Dawn' had been gone over with a fine tooth comb, but although there was a quantity of evidence to show Pellissi's connection with the black market dealings of which Corpen had accused him and to incriminate Anitra, Levistien and Syd Holman, there was nothing at all even remotely concerning X.1's organization. Whatever Pellissi had known had died with him. And the man who had fired that fatal shot had not been found. Neither was there any trace of Janice's coat. That had vanished into thin air, together with Clavering's letter.

On Monday night Dene had, after consulting Colgate-Jones, decided to return to the vicarage. There was, he thought, a chance that X.1 might attempt to clear them out of the way again if he knew where they were. But up to the present X.1 had given no sign that he still existed. Dene began to wonder whether he was clever enough to do what so many failed to do — leave well alone. He was aware that although they knew something it was very little, and that anything he might attempt could easily have the effect of adding to their knowledge. He was under the impression that the attempt to secure Stacey as a hostage had emanated from a lesser brain than X.1's. It was clever, but not clever enough for him.

And if he did leave well alone they were left with nothing — nothing except the cryptic words of the dying Clavering.

'Toothpaste.'

That was the key that would unlock the door of destruction. The signal that would start the entire scheme working. And that was the only way to stop it. To find out how the signal was to be given, and prevent it.

Dene had racked his brain until his head ached, without being able to discover how this was to be done.

Toothpaste!

How could toothpaste be used as a signal? Up and down, up and down, with a regular monotony that set Carol's nerves on edge, went Dene; from the door to the window, from the window to the door. Back and forth, back and forth . . .

'Come and sit over here for a bit,' said Colgate-Jones, breaking a long silence. 'You'll wear yourself out if you go on like that.'

Dene stopped in his ceaseless patrol and turned. 'I don't mind wearing myself out if I could only find what I'm seeking,' he said in a voice that was hoarse with fatigue. 'We've got such a little time — that's the terrible part of it. We've got such a little time . . . '

'I know,' said the vicar, 'but it's useless using up energy for nothing. Sit down and rest yourself, man.'

Dene shrugged his shoulders, came over, and flung himself into a chair.

'It's a tremendous responsibility,' he muttered, pulling a pipe from his pocket and beginning to load it from his pouch with nervous fingers. 'Unless we're successful it may lead to the deaths of thousands of men . . . '

Colgate-Jones looked at him.

'You mean the Second Front?' he asked.

'I mean,' said Dene, returning his look, 'that the timing of the blow — if it is struck — couldn't be more perfect. That's all I'm at liberty to say.'

'I see.' Colgate-Jones nodded thoughtfully. 'I thought that's what it was from the first.'

'Any disorganization might prove fatal,'

went on Dene. 'Although I don't think it would have the disastrous effect that X.1 foreshadowed, it could cause incalculable damage and chaos at a time when everything *must* go smoothly.'

He lit his pipe and threw the used match into the fire.

'So you see how serious it is?' he went on, puffing out clouds of smoke. 'Somehow or other we've got to find out what Clavering meant by his reference to 'toothpaste'.'

'However this signal is given,' said Stacey, 'it must be in such a way that will reach all the people concerned at the same moment . . . '

'But what way?' interrupted Dene. 'What way? How can toothpaste be used to reach people all over the country at the same time?'

'Could it be something over the radio?' suggested Carol. 'That would reach everybody, and . . . '

'I've thought of that,' said Dene, shaking his head. 'And I've been on to the B.B.C. They say that none of their programmes for the next month contain any reference, directly or indirectly, to toothpaste.'

'It might be a private transmitting station,' said Colgate-Jones.

'That would mean that everybody concerned would have to be given the wavelength it was operating on,' objected Dene. 'I've thought of that, too, and I am under the impression that it would be too complicated and dangerous. A transmitting station can be detected . . .'

'Supposing it is being sent from Germany?' said Carol. 'That would reach everybody . . .'

'Hamburg,' said Stacey with a smile. 'Do you remember the old programmes? 'This is the Rinso hour. Soak your clothes the Rinso way and stop feeling tired on washing day. This programme comes to you by courtesy of Rinso . . . ''

He broke off as Michael Dene leapt to his feet, his pipe falling to the floor amid a shower of burning tobacco.

'That's it!' he cried excitedly. 'I believe you've hit it! Toothpaste . . . advertising . . .'

'The Hamburg station doesn't do that

now . . . ' said Stacey.

'I know that!' snapped Dene. 'But the *newspapers still carry adverts*. Here . . . give me the papers!'

Colgate-Jones picked up three from the floor beside his chair and held them out. Dene almost snatched them from his hand, and rapidly turned the pages, while the others crowded round him excitedly.

'Most of the firms who advertise extensively are well-established British . . . ' began Colgate-Jones doubtfully.

'But the *agents* who handle the advertising may not be,' said Dene, 'or at least some of their staff may not . . . Here we are: 'Snowhite for the teeth. Use Snowhite every day and chase the blackout gloom away.' That's one — here's another: 'Safety first. Keep your teeth white with Pearl Powder. Fragrant, refreshing, and antiseptic!'

He flung away the papers and strode over to the telephone. Colgate-Jones was not on the dialling system and he called exchange.

'Hello,' he said, tapping the hook

impatiently. 'Get me Central 65902, please.'

He waited for the connection, drumming on the desk with his fingertips. Two round, hectic spots of colour burned in his pale cheeks, and there was a dry glitter in his eyes.

'Is that the *Megaphone*?' he asked, as the connection was made. 'Put me on to Mr. Corbett, will you? . . . Is that you, Corbett? Dene . . . No . . . Michael Dene. Dene! D.E.N.E . . . Yes . . . Look here, I want to speak to one of your reporters — Lawson, Dick Lawson. Yes, it is — very.' There was a further interval of impatient drumming on the desk, and then: 'Lawson? This is Dene. How are you, old man? Oh, fine . . . Listen, I want you to get me some information. Who are the agents who supply the copy for the standard toothpaste ads that appear regularly in the newspapers? Snowhite and Pearl Powder . . . Well, you can ring me back — Claybury 340, and Lawson . . . when would the copy for an ad on Saturday reach the office? Oh, I see. Be as quick as you can in calling back, will you, old chap? It's urgent. Thanks.'

He hung up, and looked at the expectant faces of the others.

'I wonder if I'm right?' he said. 'I think I am — I hope I am.'

He picked up his pipe and fingered it absently. Nobody said anything. They were all waiting for the ring of the telephone, and presently it came.

'Hello,' said Dene. 'Just a minute.' He picked up a pencil. 'All right, go ahead, Lawson . . . Only two . . . Yes . . . ' He scribbled rapidly on a scrap of paper. ' . . . I've got that . . . and . . . O.K . . . They are the only two? Thanks a lot, Lawson Now put me on to your advertising manager, will you?'

There was a short interval of silence and then:

'Good morning. My name is Michael Dene.' He explained briefly who he was. 'Could you tell me if any space has been requisitioned in your paper for an advertisement for toothpaste in Saturday's issue? . . . Both for Snowhite and Pearl Powder? Have you got the copy for the ads from the agents? . . . Thanks, I'll be coming along to see you right away. About an hour . . . It's urgent Government business. Yes . . . yes . . . goodbye.'

He turned away from the telephone.

'I'm going up to town,' he said briefly, and was at the door before they had a chance to say a word.

'Here, just a moment!' exclaimed Colgate-Jones indignantly. 'You're not going on your own. We're coming . . . '

'Hurry up, then!' called Dene from the hall. 'I'm leaving now.'

It was a breathless crowd that tumbled into the back of Dene's car a few seconds later, and four rather white-faced people who got out when the car stopped later before a big building in Fleet Street.

'I'm glad we've got here alive!' grunted Colgate-Jones, wiping his damp face.

'I never thought we should,' whispered Carol. 'That corner — at the cross-roads . . . '

'Holy smoke!' breathed Stacey. 'That was some going!'

Janice said nothing. She was still too breathless.

'You'd better wait in the waiting-room,'

said Dene as they entered the offices of the *Megaphone*. 'I won't be long.'

He hurried away, and he was gone for nearly twenty minutes. When he returned they saw at once that he had made a discovery.

'It wasn't Pearl Powder,' he said shortly. 'I've seen the Pearl Powder advert and there's nothing in it that could possibly form a message. Besides, they tell me it hasn't been changed for a long time. Come on.'

'Where are we going now?' demanded Colgate-Jones, as Dene led the way out to the street.

'To XYZ Advertising Agency,' answered Dene curtly. 'They handle 'Snowhite'. Their adverts haven't changed either — *until the one for Saturday's issue*.'

Stacey whistled.

'How do you know?' he asked.

'I've seen the copy,' answered Dene. 'It hasn't been changed much — just two lines — but they are significant enough, knowing what we know. They've been inserted in a 'box' — 'Buy your tube of Snowhite on your way home tonight.'

'Tonight' is in italics.'

Colgate-Jones uttered an exclamation.

'*That* seems plain enough,' he said, and Dene nodded.

His eyes were bright and all the tiredness and weariness had left his face.

'I think it is,' he said. 'I haven't any doubt that it's the signal from X.1 which Clavering was trying to tell you before he died. What I'm wondering now is — shall we find X.1 at the advertising office?'

26

Tuesday — 2 p.m.

Mr. Horace Smith, who was known to the Third Reich as Y.3, sat behind his large desk in his private office at XYZ Advertising Agency and his red, genial face was a little worried and strained.

There was a lot of work waiting for his attention, but his mind was occupied with other things, and it lay on his littered table unheeded. The remains of the lunch, which he had had sent in that day, were on a tray at his elbow, and the fact that he had eaten scarcely any of it testified to the extent of his perturbation — for Mr. Smith was usually very fond of his food.

And he was very worried indeed.

It had been his own idea to secure Stacey as a hostage, and the plan had not only failed, but it had resulted in three of his best agents having been caught. He was not afraid that they would talk, but he needed their services now more than ever before, when all the plans and careful preparations, which had taken so long to perfect, were about to come to fruition.

The advertising office, which, by the way, was quite a legitimate and very profitable business, had been of great service. X.1 had seen its possibilities from the beginning and exploited them to the full. It had been the general post office of the Nazi group. Through the advertisements which it handled, all kinds of messages and instructions had been transmitted to their various agents throughout the country.

It was easy for Mr. Smith to suggest little additions and alterations to the copy which his clients supplied, and in the majority of cases it was even left to him to suggest the wording and layouts. It was in this way that all instructions and communications were carried out with X.1, whom Mr. Smith had never seen, although he was his second in command.

Mr. Smith helped himself to a cigar and smoked thoughtfully. The tobacco soothed his nerves, and today they needed soothing, for he had an unusual feeling of unease.

He put this down to the failure of his plan on the previous night and lack of sleep, for he had not retired to bed until after four o'clock and had been up again just after seven. It was impossible that anything could go wrong in the big scheme. Everything was ready, and the signal had already been incorporated in the Saturday advert for 'Snowhite toothpaste'.

That would tell one hundred section leaders in charge of operations that the time had come. It was simple and foolproof. That was X.1's genius.

Mr. Smith delicately deposited a cone of ash from his cigar in an ashtray on his desk and eyed the mass of work that waited his attention. He really must get down to it, he thought. It would never do to neglect his legitimate job. He sighed and pulled some proofs towards him. He had just unscrewed the cap from his fountain-pen when there was a tap on the door and his secretary came in.

She was an elderly woman, and she carried in her hand a card.

'Will you see this gentleman, sir?' she said. 'He states that his business is urgent.'

'I'm very busy,' murmured Mr. Smith. 'What does . . . ' He broke off and his stomach gave a queer internal twitch as he read the name on the card which she laid in front of him.

MR. MICHAEL DENE

For a moment he felt a wave of panic flow over him and it seemed as if all the blood in his body had suddenly drained to his feet. He must, indeed, have gone white, for his secretary said with alarm:

'What's the matter, sir? Aren't you feeling well?'

'Yes, yes,' said Mr. Smith hastily. 'I'm all right — quite all right — just a momentary twinge of — of rheumatism — that's all. I'll see this gentleman.'

The woman went away and Mr. Smith braced himself for the coming interview. What did it mean — this visit? Dene must have discovered something to have brought him here . . .

The door opened and his secretary ushered Dene into the office.

'Good morning,' said Mr. Smith. 'Sit down, Mr. — er — Dene, please, and tell me what I can do for you.'

'Thank you,' said Dene, but remained standing. 'You are Mr. Smith, I believe?'

Mr. Smith nodded.

'And you own this agency?' continued Dene.

'I do,' replied Mr. Smith, and managed to force an expression of astonishment into his face. 'May I inquire the reason for these rather extraordinary questions?'

'You may,' snapped Dene curtly. 'Three men were arrested last night, Smith, who were German agents working for the Third Reich. This morning they made a complete statement which incriminates you . . . Keep your hand away from that drawer!'

Mr. Smith found himself staring into the round, black muzzle of an automatic which covered him steadily. The hand which he had moved stealthily towards the drawer in his desk, where he kept a revolver in case of emergency, stiffened. The game was up and he knew it. If his agents had talked there was no hope.

'Keep still,' said Dene, and called: 'Colgate-Jones.'

The vicar, his face beaming with excitement, came hurriedly in.

'Telephone the police,' said Dene without taking his eyes off the man behind the desk. 'Tell them to come here as quickly as they can.'

Mr. Horace Smith, who was known to the Third Reich as Y.3, sat in despairing silence.

★ ★ ★

No documents of any kind relative to the Nazi group were found in the offices of XYZ Advertising Agency, although the police made a thorough and extensive search, watched by the astonished and whispering staff. But at Mr. Horace Smith's small suburban villa there was more than sufficient evidence to justify his arrest. Here the table, with its large map was discovered, and in a cleverly concealed hiding-place under the floor of the sitting room was found a large collection of documents and, what was more valuable to Dene than anything else, a thick, leather-bound book containing the names and addresses of all the people working for the group. Here also was a detailed outline of the scheme which Clavering had given his life to stop.

While Dene studied this amazing document, the telephone wires hummed and the police of every county, town and village swooped, making wholesale arrests.

By the following day 45,000 people had been taken into custody, testifying to the extent of X.1's organization. They were not all of German origin. The majority were people with a grievance against society at large and the British Government in particular.

These fanatics had been cleverly roped in, and few of them even realized that they were working for the Third Reich.

The scheme itself was vast, but reduced to such a simple form that Dene, as he digested it, became more and more certain that it would have met with more than partial success.

He completed his final inspection of the documents relating to it on the Wednesday night in Colgate-Jones' study at the vicarage, and when he had finished he looked at the vicar gravely.

'It was a very good job we scotched this,' he said. 'It would have very nearly had the effect X.1 predicted if it had been carried out.'

'What was supposed to happen?' asked Colgate-Jones curiously.

'Chaos throughout the country,' said Dene. He got up and walked over to the fireplace and began to fill his pipe.

'The genius of the whole thing,' he went on, 'lay in the fact that everybody concerned would have been acting independently; each was a little cog in the giant machine without being aware that there *was* a machine. Do you understand what I mean?'

'Not quite,' admitted Colgate-Jones.

'Well,' Dene continued, 'with the exception of the section leaders, each person in this vast scheme had one *small*

318

act to perform, an act which, as far as they were aware, had no connection with anything or anybody else. Each act of itself would have produced scarcely a pinprick, but when *all* the acts took place *simultaneously* the result would have been next door to disastrous. For instance, one man in a small village in Hampshire was detailed to blow up a bridge connecting two roads. The bomb was supplied to him and full details about its fixing and the best time to fix it. That wouldn't have caused much disorganization, but when you think that this was to take place at the *same moment* to every important bridge in the country it's a different story. The same thing was to happen to sections of all the important railway tracks. The destruction of all telephone exchanges and factories were planned. In fact, to put the scheme in a nutshell, every possible component part of the war effort was to be *simultaneously* sabotaged. It is this *simultaneousness* that would have proved so disastrous. It was to be applied to everything — transport, communications, factories. The organization was perfect. Everything had been planned in detail.

Not the smallest of the little cogs was left to work on his own initiative. His instructions were complete to the last word. It must have taken a colossal amount of work.'

'But surely,' protested Colgate-Jones, 'in war-time these people with a grievance would not have done these things. They must have realized that they were putting the safety of the country in jeopardy?'

Dene looked at him steadily.

'When the miners struck,' he said, '*they* must have known that they were jeopardizing the success of the Second Front. But it didn't stop 'em, and their grievance was a personal one. No, Jones. These little men, whom X.1 was going to use for his own ends, would have thought that they were serving their own ends — getting their own back for some real or fancied wrong. There are thousands of 'em. You can hear them talking and grumbling, and they haven't the *brains* to think. That's what X.1 meant when he said such a scheme would have been impossible in any other country. You realize what it would have meant — this wholesale chaos

— these thousands of little pinpricks all happening at the same time and combining to make one huge whole? The Second Front is imminent. With transport disorganized, railways useless, it would have failed, because this was timed to take place *when it would have been too late* to cancel arrangements. It was timed for zero hour. X.1's information was very accurate.'

He finished stuffing tobacco into the bowl of his pipe and lit a match.

'Well,' he said, 'X.1's organization has been smashed in time.'

'And what about X.1?' asked Colgate-Jones.

'He remains, as he described himself, a cipher, a nothing, an unknown,' answered Dene. 'There is nothing to suggest the identity of X.1 among any of the documents and papers we found.'

27

Monday — 8.30 p.m.

'SECOND FRONT OPENS!'

'THOUSANDS OF TROOPS LAND ON FRENCH COAST.'

'CONTINUOUS BOMBING BY R.A.F. AND U.S. AIRFORCE OF INVASION AREA.'

The newspapers on that Monday morning were black with leaded type. Their headlines splashed across the front pages, outvying each other in size and sensational captions. The radio put out hourly bulletins and the entire population was a seething mass of excitement. The long-awaited moment had come, and the invasion, according to the latest reports, was successful. The air bombardment had battered down the German defences before they had had time to get them really working, and American and British troops were pouring into France.

Michael Dene, weary and exhausted with the colossal amount of work he had put in during the previous week, had accepted Colgate-Jones' invitation to spend the weekend at the vicarage, and now the clergyman knew why X.1 had chosen the date he had for the fulfilment of his scheme. The Second Front had started in the early hours of Sunday morning, and if his plan had been successful would have disorganized all the delicate arrangements for this tremendous undertaking.

Dene had spent a quiet and restful Sunday and Monday with Colgate-Jones, Carol, Stacey and Janice Gould. They followed the reports of the operations with the keenest interest, although it must be admitted that Stacey seemed to be rather more interested in Carol.

They had had dinner and were having coffee in the study, where everybody seemed to drift to automatically who stayed at the vicarage, when they were disturbed by a knock at the door.

'Who can that be?' said Colgate-Jones.

'One of your parishioners probably, Kupie,' said Carol. 'They breeze along at all hours and usually for no particular reason, just to see 'the dear vicar'. I'll go.'

She disappeared for a moment, and came back followed by Dr. Swinton.

'Hello, Jones,' he greeted, his black, gimlety eyes running round the little circle by the fire, for it was a cold June. 'I've been meaning to look you up all the week, but I've been too busy. Had to pass this way from seeing a patient and thought I'd drop in.'

'Glad to see you, Swinton,' said Colgate-Jones. 'Sit down and make yourself comfortable. Will you have coffee or a whisky and soda?'

'I'll have coffee,' said Swinton, joining them and sitting down in the chair Colgate-Jones pushed forward.

'Well, it's started, eh?'

'Yes, it's started,' said the vicar as Carol went out to get a fresh cup. 'Let's hope it will finish soon with complete victory for the Allies and that this battered old world will find peace once more.'

'Seems to be going very well at the moment,' grunted Swinton, and then: 'What really brought me here, Jones, was curiosity. I was curious to know the outcome of the peculiar business the Friday before last. What happened?'

Colgate-Jones looked at Dene, and it was Dene who answered.

'Quite a lot happened,' he said, as Carol came in with the cup and poured out coffee. He gave a carefully edited account of the events of the week, omitting the portions that he thought it was wiser to keep to themselves.

Dr. Swinton drank his coffee and listened attentively. When Dene finished he set down his cup and grunted.

'H'm,' he said, 'smart piece of work. Not often one runs up against that sort of thing, and I was interested. So you got every one of this group except the king pippin, eh? Pity. This fellow X.1 is still at large to start all over again.'

'I doubt if he could do much damage,' said Dene. 'His teeth have been drawn. He's helpless to do much without his organization behind him. He was the brain, the planner, but he had to have people to carry out his plans. One day perhaps I shall meet him . . . '

'Meet him now!' Swinton was on his feet in the centre of the room and both his hands held an automatic. 'There are times when I carry out my plans myself,' he said, 'and this is one of the times.'

They were all completely taken by surprise, and could only stare at him in dumbfounded silence.

His voice had changed, and even his appearance in some subtle way.

'Swinton!' muttered Colgate-Jones dazedly. 'You — you are X.1?'

'I am X.1,' said Swinton. 'I told you when last we met that I had lived in England for years, but you never guessed it was almost on your own doorstep.' He gave a quick laugh. 'Well, this is my final exploit. You' — he looked malignantly at Dene — 'you wrecked all my carefully prepared plans, but you won't wreck this one. My job is finished. I can do no more good for the Reich here. As you said just now, my teeth are drawn, but I have one last bite, and that is going to be a nasty one for all of you. You have destroyed my greatest piece of work and you are going to suffer for it. I came here tonight to kill you all . . . '

'What good will it do you?' asked Dene.

'It will do me no good except the satisfaction of having revenged myself for the wrecking of my schemes,' said X.1, 'and that will be a great satisfaction.'

They looked at him and they knew that he meant what he said.

'I am your execution party,' he went on with a smile, 'and when I give the order to fire I shall press the triggers of these pistols and that will be the finish . . . '

And then Janice suddenly rose up and flung herself on him. Three reports sounded almost as one and she gave a sobbing gasp. But she clung to him long enough for Dene to act. With one spring he had gripped Swinton's wrist and wrenched the automatic from his grasp before he had time to disengage himself from the girl's arms.

Janice slid to the floor and the front of her dress was red and wet.

'Look after her,' said Dene, and struck

at Swinton's other hand as he raised the pistol. The blow caught him across the knuckles and the weapon flew out of his grasp and was deftly retrieved by Stacey. Between them they secured the struggling man, binding him with their handkerchiefs for the time being.

When they came over breathlessly to Janice, whom Colgate-Jones and Carol had lifted on to the settee, her face was white but she was conscious, and although she was obviously in pain she smiled faintly.

'That was brave of you,' said Dene. 'You must have known . . .'

'Oh, yes.' Her voice was so faint they could scarcely hear. ' . . . I knew . . . but it doesn't matter . . . You see . . . I really died . . . that night you told me . . . about Jim . . .'

Her eyes closed and they thought she had gone, but after a second she opened them.

'Jim died . . . here, didn't he?' she asked in a whisper.

Dene nodded, holding his breath unconsciously.

'Yes,' he said gently, 'on that settee.'

'It . . . it isn't really . . . very difficult to die . . . ' she murmured.

Michael Dene expelled his breath slowly.

'You'd better telephone for the police to come and take Swinton away,' he said, and Stacey went over to the telephone.

THE END

We do hope that you have enjoyed reading this large print book.

Did you know that all of our titles are available for purchase?

We publish a wide range of high quality large print books including:
Romances, Mysteries, Classics
General Fiction
Non Fiction and Westerns

Special interest titles available in large print are:
The Little Oxford Dictionary
Music Book, Song Book
Hymn Book, Service Book

Also available from us courtesy of Oxford University Press:
Young Readers' Dictionary
(large print edition)
Young Readers' Thesaurus
(large print edition)

For further information or a free brochure, please contact us at:
Ulverscroft Large Print Books Ltd.,
The Green, Bradgate Road, Anstey,
Leicester, LE7 7FU, England.
Tel: (00 44) **0116 236 4325**
Fax: (00 44) **0116 234 0205**

THE GOLDEN HORNS

John Burke

In wartime Denmark, Martin Slade was a saboteur, then, in post-war Europe — a smuggler. Now, burying his past — he's a respectable journalist — going back to Denmark to cover a music festival. When he's approached by his old flame, Birgitte Holtesen, he spurns her and she, instead, ensnares an English musician, Sean Clifford. Returning home to England, Martin is attacked in his flat, which has been ransacked. Then he learns that Clifford has been murdered — and his body horribly mutilated . . .

THE POISON GANG

Derwent Steele

Young entrepreneur and inventor Dick Turner is framed for a crime he didn't commit by unscrupulous business rivals Morris and Ayres, who then blackmail him for his inventions. But Morris disappears, after publicly quarrelling with Turner. Then Ayres is murdered and Turner becomes chief suspect for the police investigation. However, when Turner's fiancée calls in the help of John Blackmore, the famous investigator, he soon discovers there's an even greater and sinister criminal conspiracy at work . . .